MW01275692

The Journey to Return

A Story of Recovery
A Book of Redemption

By Norma Luciano

ISBN: 1-4823-7438-2
ISBN-13: 9781482374384

As children bring their broken toys with tears for us to mend, I brought my broken Dreams to God because He was my Friend.

But then instead of leaving Him in peace to work alone, I hung around and tried to help With ways that were my own.

At last I snatched them back and cried, "How can you be so slow?"
"My child," He said, "What could I do? You never did let go."

—Author Unknown

Journey: A Story of Recovery

Table of Contents

"I know that my Redeemer lives, and that in the end he will stand upon the earth. And after my skin has been destroyed, yet in my flesh I will see God."

(Job 19:25-26).

Part I
Morgan and the King

Interlude

You will have these tassels to look at and so you will remember all the commands of the LORD, that you may obey them and not prostitute yourselves by going after the lusts of your own hearts and eyes. (Numbers 15:39)

Morgan: "I hurt. This path I am on hurts ... Repeat."

Heart: "I hurt, too, and my way is to release through distraction. See; look over there. That has worked before—"

Morgan: "You're right, it has, but the price was devastating. I am not willing to pay the price again. But, oh ... it sure looks good."

Game Master: "Yes, Morgan, come back. Keep playing with me and our friends. We miss you. I know you're lonely and you hurt. This will make it all go away. Besides, everyone is being mean to you, they don't understand. No one does except me, and right here is the solution-sweet ecstasy. One drop, and you will be all better, my friend."

Heart: "Oh, Morgan, come on. This will be fun, and it will feel good. Oh, it looks so beautiful; can't you smell how delicious it will be? And yeah, people have been hard on you lately. You're a man; you don't need to stand for that. You're in charge and can prove once and for all to everyone who is boss!"

Morgan: "You guys sure present an alluring package. Wow, I am starting to feel better just considering it. Wait ... wait ... wait... What is that nauseating sensation in my guts? Something isn't right; I got to just slow down, think and remember! I have been here many times before, and nothing good ever came from this. My brain, my body, almost destroyed if not for the King—"

Heart and Game Master together: "Oh, Morgan, forget Him! He hasn't helped you yet. It's been one problem after another since He showed up. We used to have so much fun until He spoiled everything. Think back on all the great times like when you were being worked over by that bad man, and the three of us started playing with the joy drops, and—"

Morgan: "OK, you guys, *shut up*! You have gone far enough. My guts are grinding, and I feel like I am going to pass out. My King—help! I am in trouble. This is too much for me to deal with."

When he turns the light on, all the darkness with its creatures and demons scatter like cockroaches.

Still … it hurts deep. There is no outside evidence. Maybe a crease between the eyes, or a sad look. But no bandage or blood. But oh, the wound, it must hurt. Like a limb hanging by a thread or the innards hanging out, somehow able to function because life still flows in the body. It comes down to survival—the desire to live is very powerful.

Breathe even as the memories batter against the dam of the mind. Though there are many holes, somehow it doesn't collapse. Well, sometimes it becomes so excruciating, it takes over and ravages, causing the person to withdraw and disappear. They are gone, sometimes forever. Medication, professionals, institutions, often no one can penetrate the pain for that has become too dangerous.

There is no hope. Only the King can come in: Please come and heal me. Take away this torment. It is too great to bear. I must breathe, but I don't want to. Many wounded have fallen forever. "Multitudes, multitudes in the valley of decision," says the ancient Book.[1] The King has touched my heart and mind in the place where the lies control. He spoke truth so I invited him in, and He has healed me—a lifelong experience.

I know the ravages from the lies of the Game Master. He and his cronies have run my life since my first breath. Beyond my earliest memories when I was a baby, they were other people's memories. My whole life tangled in a labyrinth of lies that felt like truth was my reality far too long. One abuse after another until it seemed there was no more blood left for my veins. The brain responded to the lies as I tortured myself to the point where there was almost nothing left in me.

---

1   Joel 3:14.

Cruel people, what they did and said caused me to react by self-medicating. I wanted to escape it all but where and how? I went to the mean streets where loud, abrasive, savage-like wolves fought for that last rabbit. We who were out in the streets did horrible things to one another—howling, ripping, devouring. There was a code of honor, but only to a point. Not everyone plays by my rules. The problem is everyone has their own rules they want to play by, I guess that is the point. Hence, pain stacked on pain-I thought this would be my forever.

It defined me, and I was happy in my delicious misery. I liked those sedatives. Up, down, and all around—crazy, crazy; it was a setup. Like forever in a revolving door with no way out. There is only so much ripping and tearing one can take. Then he lashes back, just as he was taught. Hurt *hurts*, and so the cycle goes.

Wild wolves—when the Game Master runs the ship we follow blindly, helplessly. Each whim stirred up in our hearts and minds must be covered or satiated depending on how we are drawn away and enticed. Like a fish lure—thinking it is something that it is not for its reality is hidden behind beauty; that is the heart of the Game.

Many things happen which appear to be isolated incidents, having nothing to do with each other. But people and things collide. If the window is cracked, when hit, it shatters. So with people. It is the brokenness, the pain and lies that invite these unrelated incidents to impact a shattered life.

But the King uses all things to bring restoration for He wants us to be whole. The question is, do we? Waiting, hurting, lies mounting. The King is always waiting, even as I was engaging in great treachery with the Game Master. There was a sliver in time ...

Chapter 1
A Fractured Family

Well, let's not get too far ahead and overlook the life of a tortured boy transformed by a miraculous King, who later became a valiant warrior.

This precious life was born with such promise. Sure chaos was all around, but here was a new life. In the midst of a drunken house party raging around them, Mommy put down her drink long enough to give birth to baby Morgan. Only a few short months passed before the Game Master turned up the volume in this family and claimed Daddy's life.

He was found suspended from a beam at the job site. When the construction crew he worked with arrived at the home they had been building, that is how they found him. Daddy was never one to arrive earlier than necessary. He was the kind of guy to ride out every party, often until work started next morning. Even though all the evidence pointed to foul play, the investigation ceased once the detectives realized it was only Daddy. A lot of men wanted him dead, anyway-his various escapades around town, some with their wives, helped drive that decision. His death was labeled a "work-related accident," and that is the way it would stay. Those who knew him debated the truth of the matter.

Though Daddy was a ladies' man, probably the game which caused him to pay with his life, Mommy was head over heels in love with him. She didn't seem to mind his other women but behaved as though it was normal. These extras, she believed, was a small price to pay for love considering the other cruel men before Daddy. Daddy wasn't that way but was always fun loving, a party in movement. He was the kind of guy that could cause a dead man to sit up and laugh during his own funeral. Though sounding farfetched, those who knew Daddy knew that kind of gallows humor was near true. Thus, when he died, Mommy did, too. Her body continued breathing, eating, functioning, though just barely. Mostly she was gone, lost in grief. What were previously celebrations became Mommy's opportunity to turn into festivals of mourning.

She had four young children and now baby Morgan. Diapers, bottles, while the bigger ones ran circles around her. It was too much to take. They soon realized if they were to survive, the older ones must take matters into their own hands, which they did. Actually, most of the responsibility was met by the eldest daughter, who was just twelve years old. Even when Daddy was alive, she had grown-up responsibilities that left their dirty stain on her tender heart. But she couldn't think or feel these things; a job had to be done to raise the little ones, and that she did. Years later, she still is trying to wash those stains from her memory, trapped in the Game Master's web of lies. It was sad for Sissy, actually sad for us all. Everyone ends up paying.

At twelve, Sissy was not equipped to be a mommy, but she did her best. Mommy herself became the little girl. This helped to train the cycle of destruction to her young ones. She was so permissive; they even participated in the drunken festivals with Mommy. "No." That word did not exist in Mommy's vocabulary. "Let the kids do as they want." Again, Sissy had to be the tough one and the younger ones would cower before her. She always used her fist or her raised hand. That is why no one asked Sissy. Instead, they went to Mommy. Even the young ones knew how to get what they wanted.

Since there was so little of everything to go around including Mommy's love, the little ones hungered immensely. As a result, baby Morgan was viewed as the enemy by his older siblings. Mommy tended to give him more affection since he never knew Daddy, and he was Daddy's last baby; she never meant any harm. From the time of Daddy's death, the others would find different ways to torment Morgan. Though they didn't mean to be cruel, Mommy was so absent and Sissy so broken that they ended up acting out of sheer instinct from their own pain and neglect. Just a reminder, hurt hurts.

Over the formative years of Morgan's childhood, Mommy started to heal from her position of grieving widow, though never fully recovering. Off to work she went, yet constantly struggling with poverty. Mommy was an energetic worker, but the minimum wage she made barely covered their provisions. Thankfully, the church and the state stepped in. But you know, institutional breakfasts—lumpy bumpy oatmeal along with many grumpy adults who were sometimes not the kind workers they should have been.

After her time of mourning, Mommy did her best to support her hungry crew. Unfortunately, an incomplete education and few skills brought her to only degrading low wage jobs. She tried to balance her personal need for pleasure and practical need for survival as a Mommy of five, but that didn't go over so well for she didn't always make the best choices.

She would sometimes be missing for nights on end. One time Morgan's older brother went looking for her. After going from restaurant to nightclub, he found her dancing on stage. A young child should not have had to look for his mother in such places. Before long, the authorities found out and took all the little ones away from Mommy. They told her, "Only a short while. Maybe in a couple of years so you'll grow up." And so, Morgan and the rest of the children were put in various "homes."

Chapter 2
Forced to Work

As for Morgan and his brothers, they were put to work in what was supposed to bea foster home. No, not house chores, but the drug trade. Since they were placed in a tough neighborhood, the authorities wouldn't check those children's homes too well. It looked quite normal from the outside, but there were lots of secrets within. A hidden door when opened revealed an enclosed concrete basement. Morgan's house parents had about twenty kids who were supposedly rescued from unsafe situations. They were put to work in the lucrative drug trade, from manufacturing to distributing.

Morgan had been just six years old when taken from his mother and moved across the country to this far away nightmare. He was too small to do much so his tasks were to sweep and mop the floors and empty the garbage cans regularly. The kids weren't allowed to pollute the drugs. That's why the guards checked everything, to make sure no one was stealing them, which included little Morgan. Whenever he took out the trash, they searched him very carefully. The goal was profit so they would keep the boys humiliated and attentive to make sure there were no drugs on them.

The house parents had a couple adult children of their own who helped run the business. As soon as the kids would awaken, they were put straight to work. School was not remotely important to the house parents and they wouldn't send the kids whenever the authorities weren't looking. They slowly hooked them on drugs to keep them working harder; they had to be careful how they did things. They didn't need the authorities snooping around, not that they ever did.

School was not supportive, either. Overworked teachers grew discouraged from years of attempting to teach people who refused to change. From time to time a young enthusiastic teacher would arrive but would soon become disabled by a community consumed with its commitment to its ways of doing things. The attitude in the community was, kids are to be worked and not heard.

Mommy, on the other hand, was trying to get her life right and get her kids back, but where could she find justice? No one would listen, for this family was deemed of no consequence. Mommy, a widow with five children, had little means and even less power; besides, she struggled with her own demons.

As a result, Morgan and kids like him tried to survive on their own wits. Morgan escaped oftento the lower foothills of the semiarid desert set above the lush farmlands where he stayed. There, he heard and sometimes saw wild wolves along with snakes and scorpions dotting the terrain, and learned to be very careful where he stepped. Occasionally his friend James would join him and they would pretend to be free.

On one of those escapades in the foothills, James came within strike zone of a coiled rattler. Morgan was further back and coached James not to look at the snake, but follow his cue. "Run!" yelled Morgan, and James sure did. Morgan hit the snake in the head with a big rock, then cut off the dead snake's rattles and gave them to James. "Sometimes you gotta run. But sometimes you gotta stay and fight," said Morgan. "This is to remind you to not fear your enemy." The boys made a fire and ate that roast snake to celebrate their victory.

During the times they ran away, Morgan and James weren't much missed. Between school and home, they practiced reappearing without notice. They came back to eat so they wouldn't get caught, but Morgan was always looking for a permanent escape. He stole a little knife from the kitchen, matches, and a rubber band to make a sling shot. He used a strong Y-branch from outside as a hunting tool and with practice over time he could hit all kinds of things, critters too, which he cooked over a campfire and ate.

One day he planned to run away and never return. He saw what happened to the kids who stayed (including his own brothers) and how they became part of the nightmare. He sure didn't want that to happen to him.

The house parents would "graduate" them from school and home manufacturing to street dealing and even prostitution in order to earn money for the house parents their whole lives. Hook, line and sinker, it was a messy business filled with violence and deceit. Though life at the house was harsh, the streets were worse. The kids were accustomed to being manipulated by others, although ultimately, the Game Master was behind it all.

Morgan told himself that wasn't going to happen to him. No way, he was going home. The whole family would be reunited with Mommy, all of them. Morgan would find her and convince her to get them out of there even though it was years since he had seen her. The children had been moved far away a long time ago and it seemed there wasn't any rush to reunite them. He remembered very little about Mommy since he couldn't communicate with any of the family and was just a child when moved to this place.

The guardians strictly kept all the kids from interaction. Communication would give the kids power, and they were never to be allowed that luxury. These kids were groomed to be drones, workers that must be kept weak. Violence and beatings were common occurrences. Thankfully, James was long gone, having been returned to his family. His mom was working and had been clean; his dad had been released from prison after being convicted for petty theft and drug dealing. As a result, the state reunited this family.

Morgan didn't hear from James after he left. Even if he tried, both boys knew there was no way they could contact each other, the house parents would never let any correspondence through. Morgan had memorized James's address, planning to one day visit him.

By the time Morgan turned thirteen, the vile underworld was deeply etched in his mind, having experienced street life and dealing himself. His oldest brother, hooked by the system was working the streets. Sissy never came to this place; besides, she didn't know where it was. The state had placed her and his other sister in a girls' orphanage, while the three boys were sent to this so-called "boy's home."

Morgan longed to find safety with his brothers, wanting them to escape with him, yet concerned of the consequences if they were caught. On occasion a child escaped, and when caught, as they always were, the rest of them could hear the screams coming through the walls. After a while a car would drive up and take him away, never to be heard from again. The thugs then taunted the remaining kids for months with the awful horror stories they told.

Morgan carefully planned his escape for a long time and knew he must go alone to be successful. Besides, if he was caught he couldn't bear to think of another person's harm being his responsibility. If he got away, he would report this place and the authorities would send a rescue party to set everyone free; he just knew it.

On Sundays after the late night shift was over, the thugs were usually sound asleep, exhausted from weekend parties they indulged in. Morgan had cured plenty of snake meat as part of his escape plan to distract the dogs as he went by so they would neither bark nor bite. If they caught him—well, it wasn't an option to think that.

The rainy season was now over, although nighttime was still cool. Morgan dressed quickly in jeans, a long sleeve shirt, boots and jacket. Definitely warm enough, he stuffed his pillows under the blankets to look like he was still in bed in case they checked, and gingerly walked up the steps. Stopping to listen, all he heard were loud snores.

As he came closer to the door leading outside, the dogs started to growl, crouching and ready to attack but Morgan was ready for them. He looked them straight in the eye as he spoke quietly to them, just like the adults who tended them. "Spike, Mutt, fetch," he commanded. At that he waved the dried meat for them to smell and then threw it away from the only door leading outside. As planned, the dogs went after the meat. It was dry and tough, keeping them focused on chomping the meat instead of him. While they were busy eating, he greased the door with a little soap he had saved just for this occasion. That squeaky door intended to wake up the guards had caused many an escapee's capture, and he made sure he wasn't going to be one of them.

Slowly he opened the door and slipped out without a sound, disappearing into the moonless night. Not once did he look back, avoiding neighborhood streets and then heading straight to an old tunnel that led to an abandoned coal mine in the foothills. There Morgan had hidden under a pile of rocks by the entrance a coffee can that contained his hunting tools, rag, and matches.

Putting the rag on a pole he lit it as a torch in order to see where he was going in the pitch-dark mine. Morgan moved quickly, knowing there were only a few hours before everyone woke up. He hoped his years of waking late and sneaking off to school or the hills would buy him extra time. He had to be long gone before anyone noticed him missing—he needed every opportunity to succeed. There wouldn't be a second chance if he was caught.

Morgan learned a lot about terrain and weather patterns in geography class on the infrequent days he went to school, and paid close attention to his teachers during those lessons. There were many miles to travel and he must remain safe and undetected the whole way; he needed all the help he could get. Whenever he heard any information that improved his survival skills he forced himself to sit up and listen closely, though usually exhausted from the crazy schedule forced on him.

This moonless evening, as Morgan moved quickly through the darkness, he had one destination on his mind. That destination was Mommy.

Chapter 3
Charlie's Life

The last he had heard, Mommy was still living in the same town where he was born, so that's where he headed. Morgan had charted this route for a long while, becoming familiar with the course from a map he kept in his knapsack prepared for his trek from the Midwest to the rich fertile lowlands of home on the West Coast.

The night sky was being chased away as the dawn started to break and if all went as planned, he still had a couple more hours before the house adults would awaken for the day.

Funny. I hear the sound of horse hooves, he told himself, after walking a while, and it seemed they were getting closer. He tried to comfort himself with the fact that no one at the house rode horses and hadn't used a posse when other kids escaped.

It had been hard going and Morgan was a bit winded. A break would do him good. Hiding for a while was a good idea, too, and he knew of a good spot ahead. His mind was racing as he hurriedly hid to wait out the possible threat. Those horses seemed to be getting closer with each passing moment, yet Morgan kept his wits while crouching low in the underbrush.

The horse's rider arrived and stopped right in front of him. Morgan considered his options: wait this out and hope the person would pass or jump the guy and take the horse. He could sure use one and though he didn't know how to ride, he could learn real quick.

Pondering the options, he heard a familiar voice whisper his name through clenched teeth. "Morgan, are you in there?" It sounded like his middle brother Charlie.

Morgan peered through the brush into the semi dawn. Sure enough, it was Charlie with two horses. How could this be? Morgan quickly untangled himself from his hiding place to greet his brother. Laughing, they embraced each other. Charlie instructed Morgan to put his stuff on the second horse and ride. Not only would the thugs from the boy's home be looking for the two brothers, but the folks he stole the horses from weren't gonna be too happy once they found their horses were missing.

Morgan watched the neighbors with their horses when walking to and from school, but didn't know Charlie could ride. Morgan's mind was reeling with questions; how did his brother know of his escape? How did he get the horses, or learn to ride, for that matter? How did Charlie find him? If Charlie could find him, that meant others could, too.

Interrupting Morgan's racing thoughts, Charlie got off his horse to give his brother a boost up, and Morgan got a crash course in horseback riding. There wasn't even time to be nervous. The horses had been running hard as Charlie followed Morgan's tracks. After this short rest, they were ready for the green youngster.

Charlie walked the horses in large circles the area of a football field before riding toward the foothills. About every mile the brothers made false tracks with short starts in differing directions, and then resumed their route. Since rainy season had almost passed, there were plenty of creeks flowing with fresh runoff where Charlie allowed the horses a chance to drink while catching their breath.

Taking them through the stream to set the trackers off, they disappeared into the lowland trees. Charlie seemed prepared for this escape, apparently having attained survival skills of his own. Right now his task was to shake off those trackers and their dogs, he must be thorough.

Morgan followed his brother in amazement. All this time he had done his best to hide his escape to protect the other boys, yet somehow Charlie planned this flawless escape simultaneously. The brothers ran the horses hard from the nightmare of abuses, the way only tortured captives can.

Pushing their steeds to full capacity, they stopped occasionally to rest so the horses wouldn't collapse. The terrain was changing, and the trees had become denser. They pressed on all day, well into the night before stopping to rest briefly. Getting what little light they had from the stars, they resumed their pace through the mountain pass. Thankfully, they were young and energetic and being caught was not an option.

Charlie didn't need to remind Morgan that there was plenty of interest back in the devil town to find them. It wasn't just the thugs at the drug house who wanted them—everyone wanted to get their hands on those "horse-rustling thieves." The owners wanted their horses, and if the boys couldn't be found, they would slip a report to the authorities about what was really going on in that boys' home. They threatened the house parents that if they didn't get back their valuable animals and gear Charlie had stolen, the house parents would pay. "You better believe there's a full search going on," Charlie said.

But Charlie had been smart having covered their tracks well. Taking branches, he swept Morgan's footsteps leading to the underground tunnel, which was actually how he found his brother in the first place. Charlie then took the horses a different way to the mine on many paths before they met up to buy some time. The rivers and paths they followed helped, and then came a heavy rainstorm which totally erased everything, though sloshing through the mud was slowing them down.

Empty handed, the posse must have returned to that cruel town, because the boys didn't see or hear anyone following them anymore. The authorities would place a "Wanted Dead or Alive" poster everywhere, offering money for the two young horse rustlers. They knew that in spite of the payoff money demanded from the house parents by the horses' owners, it wouldn't cover the boys' escape. No amount was enough for a successful one, and if the truth ever got out about what was going on there with the abuses to those kids, it would cause a big problem.

Exposing what was going on at the house was exactly what Charlie and Morgan intended to do. They rode hard not only to save their own skins, but all those left behind at that house. Even though their trail had been erased they had to stay out of view; this mission was too important to risk.

Skirting the forest and mountains past the desert heading west, then north through the Americas to avoid the snowy mountains, the brothers stayed in the wilderness at mid-tree line. They stopped just long enough to cook fresh game over a fire and get a few hours' sleep. Morgan had become an expert with his slingshot and knife, catching and cleaning their game. Whatever meat was left, he smoked it up real tough, preserving it so they could pull the meat out of their packs as they rode.

The weather was on their side once that first rain passed, but in the distance, dark clouds appeared clustering up mean-like. They looked like they were carrying in a mighty rough storm. The two boys watched, thinking to themselves, as they were not accustomed to talking much.

Pressing on, they looked for suitable shelter. Morgan hoped to catch something to eat while sitting out the storm, but time was running out. It was only a few hours before that storm would break, and they had to have safe shelter. Charlie and Morgan passed a couple possibilities, a fallen tree, then a cave, but neither was big enough for both them and the horses.

The first crack of thunder and bolts of lightning spooked the horses, but the boys held on. Right then Morgan spotted the perfect rabbit, and wanting fresh meat he followed the creature as it scampered away. Once he had a good shot, he took it, with Charlie following close behind.

As Morgan dismounted to gather his catch, he thought he saw a log house through the brush. *Surprising. I haven't noticed any other homes around here.* He beckoned Charlie over to hold the reins of his horse, and then held his hand up to give the quiet signal while soundlessly approaching the cabin. It appeared deserted, but he couldn't be sure.

No smoke was coming from the chimney—that was a good sign. Cobwebs covered the porch and door, suggesting no one had been around for a while. Before crossing the tree line where he was, Morgan looked both directions, fully alert for any sign of life, and then ran toward the front door.

Silently he walked up the steps and turned the doorknob. It squeaked loudly. He hoped no one was inside aiming a shotgun at him. Standing to the side of the doorjamb just in case, he peered into the dimly lit room; nothing. Waiting, he listened, and then slowly entered the front door into what appeared to be the main room. Cobwebs and more dust, both good signs the house was deserted. First he checked downstairs, then upstairs where the bedrooms were, nobody. *This must a summer cabin.* Canned goods, fully stocked and furnished, jackpot!

Going to the front door, he whistled the all clear to his brother. Out back, they found a shed and after going through it, figured the owners used it for storage when they came to stay. It was a perfect shelter to keep the horses safe from the storm.

Charlie had some oats for just such an emergency and went straight to feed, water and settle the horses in. Meanwhile, Morgan dressed the rabbit and buried the offal so as not to tempt wild animals to come their way. Gathering up some cut wood sheltered by the overhang at the side of the shed, he went inside to start a roaring fire in the wood stove.

Once the horses were tended to, Charlie brought the bags into the house and found some empty jugs and buckets for water. He went to fill them, pumping water from the well out back. He returned just as the first rain started to fall amidst the loud cracks of thunder and flashes of lightening.

The fire was crackling down to a steady burn, almost ready for frying up the rabbit in some lard and salt with the iron pan from the kitchen cupboard. Morgan also found some coffee and added a pot of water to the top of the stove to boil up.

It was getting pretty dark outside, so they lit the candles and lanterns they found in the cabin. While Morgan prepared dinner, Charlie found a broom and began knocking down the cobwebs. Rather than sleep in the bedrooms upstairs, he brought some blankets and pillows down to the main room so they could keep warm by the wood stove.

It was necessary to be close to the exit in case anyone showed up, and they kept the packed saddlebags next to their bedrolls. Charlie planned an escape route to the shed: quickly saddle, mount up, and then disappear into the nearby forest.

As the evening wore on, after devouring the meat and coffee along with some canned beans and candy found in the kitchen, the two young men began to relax. Until now, they had spoken only of essentials on this pilgrimage. Now they had some time to get reacquainted since they were sacked in by the storm, having come to trust one another over the last week. Though not parted physically all those years, the house parents had planted some crazy ideas into their heads to keep them at odds with each other. Even if they did get opportunity to speak at that place, they didn't. If suggestions of distrust weren't enough, the consequential beatings kept them divided. Morgan had scars to prove it from his earlier friendship with James.

Sitting contentedly before the fire, Morgan's thoughts drifted toward James. Though he lived on their route home, Morgan must deal with his own uncertain situation before visiting his friend. He trusted James, but was unsure about anyone else. What if someone reported him and Charlie to the authorities? He wouldn't start that line of thinking. Though part of his original plan had not included the horses and Charlie, now it was impossible to think of leaving them.

Morgan had a lot of questions for his middle brother, and it was time they talk. Until now, they had been pretty lucky, but they still had a few weeks' steady ride ahead. Besides, how did Charlie know what he knew? Two horses, the tunnel the timing with Morgan's escape, it was uncanny.

Charlie was focused on his own musings but was brought to the moment once Morgan muttered, "Hey, I got some questions that need some answers." This was to be their first real conversation with each other. Without much practice it was a slow start, but Morgan determined to learn how Charlie escaped like he did.

Charlie responded slowly. Starting at their childhood, he explained how the last five years at the drug house made him grow up quickly. Charlie became a wanderer at a very young age. As with all travelers, given many challenges, he chose the Game Master for a season, but thankfully, Wisdom finally reached him.

He had been very wild; at one point he caught untamed horses and rode them as the natives of the land had for centuries, without bit or bridle. Though almost a forgotten art it came to him easily, for this was his way, too. Throwing down all responsibility, he mounted a wild steed running full speed ahead to the most rugged countryside.

The family was broken after Daddy died. Mommy moved back to her family's home in the country, where rivers and farmlands dominated the isolated location. Never really accepted by his peers, Charlie said loneliness was one of the factors that helped push him to run so hard and so far. "I felt unrestrained, raw pain," he told Morgan with sadness in his voice. "This was one of the ways I dealt with it."

Through that open door he described how the Game Master came in, showing him all kinds of games. They were fun, and just as he rode the horses hard, that is the way he did everything. Though he formed some friendships, all too soon he found himself alone and isolated. Isolation was a habit he developed well over the years, and it became a way of life that left him vulnerable to many things. That was about the time he and his brothers were sent to foster care at the drug house.

One of the thugs there told him there was neither good nor bad, just choice. Another said all he would ever become was a bum or a wild man. Armed with these opinions, he overlooked the side effects and consequences of those choices, thus becoming very confused.

At one point in the midst of a hallucination, he found himself neck high in an inlet from the sea. He probably would have kept walking in and drowned, had it not been for those "good church folks" assembled at the shore watching. They must have been praying him out from a briny death as he somehow came to his senses and swam back to shore, never to return to that dangerous endeavor. Although never approaching those young watchers, he was safe yet again from the jaws of death

This experience along with numerous insane choices did not cause Charlie to turn to Wisdom's guidance. Instead, he wholeheartedly pursued the lovely delicacies presented by the Game Master. Trying many things, he didn't realize he was becoming deeply entangled beyond the help of human aid. Running drugs on the streets while being loaded, he soaked up sights and smells that aroused passions deep within. More, more, more ... but it seemed he couldn't find any satisfaction. Finally, he thought to end his misery by taking his own life.

That day on the streets, high, and selling drugs for the house parents, someone walked up to him and started talking about some guy named the King. It wasn't the first time, but today was different. In the past he had been so spaced out he just continued to sell. This time, for some reason he sobered up immediately and focused on every word that was said. As the guy talked, another one came almost out of nowhere saying, "The LORD himself goes before you and will be with you; he will never leave you nor forsake you. Do not be afraid; do not be discouraged." He didn't know it at the time, but the man was quoting a Scripture from Deuteronomy 31:8.

"Will you repent and receive salvation?" the man asked. Charlie figured he was as good as dead anyhow. These fellows had sparked a place of real truth within. Charlie responded, "Yup, I believe." A rush like fire surged right through him. It burned out the old, and he was brand new.

He stopped selling and using drugs right then. Each day the house parents gave him the goods; he dumped them down a public toilet and instead wandered the streets watching people. His new friends walked and talked with him some of the days, though mostly he was alone with his thoughts. The guys gave him money daily for the house parents so they wouldn't find out what was going on. They also helped him with every detail of this escape, they and the King, that is.

Charlie went on to say the two men were with him all the way, even now, from elsewhere sent to guide Morgan home. "Only you, Morgan," Charlie insisted. He went on: "My time here is very short."

Puzzled, Morgan asked, "What do you mean? How do you know that?"

But Charlie wouldn't respond to those questions. He just kept repeating, "Trust the King."

The boys waited out the storm a couple days. They spent time talking, laughing like kids should, catching up, planning. That's when Charlie introduced Morgan to the King. Morgan was filled with joy and peace for the first time in his life. As a child, he scratched and clawed for Mommy's attention. Later at the drug house, he had to watch his every move like a convict. When his brother introduced him to the King and Wisdom, Morgan was filled with newfound confidence and felt his life change radically.

The second night at the cabin, the storm blew over and they looked up to see the stars twinkling in the clear sky outside. They had been out with the horses earlier, grazing them in a grassy area close by, returning them to the shed where they were safe from wild animals—and eyes of the too-curious. Both brothers along with the horses were well fed and rested. The boys had finished the rabbit along with some canned goods from the cabin; it was time to capture fresh game. Charlie took the horses to graze one more time while Morgan hunted for dinner. He pegged a couple wild pheasants, dressed them and cooked them up. Both boys pronounced them delicious.

After eating, they packed for an early start next morning. Going around the cabin, they tidied up as best they could. Charlie wrote a thank you note to the owners and put it in the kitchen cupboard under some canned goods in case anyone checked the cabin for their whereabouts.

Ready to depart early in the morning, Charlie turned to his brother. "Keep the faith. Don't be confused by what you see or feel. Promise me no matter what, you will stay close to the King."

Morgan muttered, "OK, whatever," and then rolled over. As he fell asleep, he half heard Charlie talking with Wisdom and the King. Charlie cried, "Please keep Morgan close, you promised. Don't leave him. I trust you ..." Then all was still.

Morgan woke up first. He reached over to give Charlie a tap on the shoulder. They got up, put their blankets upstairs where they had found them, and finished the left over pheasant. Giving a last glance around the cabin, they closed the door behind them, saddled the horses, and off they went.

Things went smoothly for the remainder of the trek north. They mostly traveled the mountain range and from then on found plenty of game to hunt. The weather was often overcast, although there wasn't much rain, which suited the brothers. They talked about everything, for they felt safe with each other.

Over the last month they covered a lot of territory while staying out of sight. Their destination was getting close. The morning arrived when Charlie told Morgan that day, they were going home. "You are to go on without me," Charlie said.

By now, Morgan was used to his brother's unusual comments. Shrugging his shoulders, he left it at that.He knew he wouldn't get any more information from Charlie, anyhow.

They broke camp as usual, but before mounting the horses Charlie put his arm around Morgan's neck and whispered roughly, "I love you. Don't worry, all is well. We'll see each other soon enough. Serve the King the whole way until... There is a word from the King to you.

"Stand at the crossroads and look; ask for the ancient paths, ask where the good way is, and walk in it, and you will find rest for your souls." [2]

They would arrive home within a few hours. The two brothers were grateful they had come to love and accept one another for who they were. This precious gift was forged in the fire of affliction they had walked together.

It seemed the perilous journey to get back home was almost over and Morgan chattered the whole way. Filled with anticipation for his reunion with Mommy, he was overcome with excitement.

Charlie, on the other hand, was aloof. It wasn't unusual for him to wait and consider what he wanted to say before he spoke, but today he paused longer than usual wanting each word to count. This special morning as the sun came up bright and clear, all creation appeared to be celebrating the upcoming family reunion. Anyone else would have considered it a perfect day to return home, but not Charlie.

Finally Charlie broke his silence while Morgan listened with rapt attention. Slowly listing the instructions again, Charlie unfolded the plans of their descent into the valley and then home. At each point, Charlie quizzed his little brother, making sure every detail was

2   From the Holy Book, Jeremiah 6:16.

memorized and in order. "You must follow each point exactly as I've directed," he said. Morgan heard the whole plan again, repeating it back to his brother. When he was done, he stopped and waited, for the conversation seemed incomplete.

After an uncomfortable silence Charlie spoke, "Truth, little brother—receive and live it exclusively. There shall be many distractions over your days on earth, but remember the details of our return. I heard the King say that as He brought us this far safely, so He will fulfill His every promise.

"When you see Mommy, tell her I love her and let her know I went home today. Tell everyone you meet about the King. In the process of exposing those at the drug house, keep in mind He wants them to give all that up and turn to Him instead. Sure, it is hard, I mean look at all we've been through—life is multidimensional. Don't get lost seeing through your own limited vision. Instead, ask the King to give you His perspective for His truth will set you free. No matter what happens when we get to the valley, don't look back or slow down. You will know the time, and then run your steed as hard as he will go. Promise me this, and remember to remember."

Both young men and horses were rested and refueled. Standing together, Morgan's memory played over the last month crossing that rugged terrain. There had been trials, but also blessings, and laughter. The most amazing gift was meeting his new friends, Wisdom and the King.

Ready to mount the horses, they caught each other's gaze. Morgan felt strangely overcome with emotions of pure love coming from his brother. He had no recollection of this feeling. *To have a brother like Charlie who has no agenda other than love—wow, it is otherworldly.* The counsel his brother gave to allow the love received from the King to be embroidered into his heart then share it with others was worth consideration.

Before descending into the valley, Charlie shook Morgan's hand and embraced him again saying, "I love you."

As soon as they started riding, the atmosphere seemed to change. Both brothers needed to focus intently on the King's instructions: "OK, steady trot, the sun is three-fourths of the way up from the highest mountain peak to the east. That means it's almost noon, head to the north side of town past Central, 4401 Plank Street, and home. Focus on the details, they are very important."

Less than a half mile from town, they noticed people milling around, though some were working their farms. There were sounds drifting from a nearby tavern, a door slammed shut, loud voices, men shouting ...

"Run!" yelled Charlie.

Although his adrenaline was pumping full force, Morgan followed Charlie's instructions and ran his horse with all his might. He heard a lot of commotion behind him, but didn't look back just as Charlie had told him. It seemed his heart was pounding to the rhythm of the horses' hoof beats.

He sensed it before hearing it, as his heart was about to pound out. *Bang*!

Chapter 4
A Return Filled with Danger

"Don't look back, don't look back," echoed in Morgan's head from Charlie's instructions. Charlie's strange behavior and the King's instructions were starting to make sense. His brain wouldn't think. Focus! "4401 Plank Street, 4401 Plank Street," he kept repeating, *Run hard, even if the guts fall out of the horse—just don't look back.* Dodging in and out of the trees, he noted the sounds behind him were starting to fade. Now there was just the steady rhythm of his horse's hoof beats beneath him.

This should have been comforting having lost the pursuers. It wasn't, because he no longer heard his brother's horse behind him. Still, he kept pressing forward, though his horse was panting and frothing at the mouth. Morgan had to get to Mommy, she had to be home. Would someone arrest him when he got there? He put those thoughts out of his mind. "Just do as Charlie said," he told himself.

Almost there, he slowed his steed to a gentle run to cool down some. Central, Front, Lisp, there's Plank. Follow the next instructions: *Stop long enough to remove your things from the horse, put a rock under the saddle, and slap the horse hard on the rump. The horse will run far and fast to get away from that rock, leading away the folks pursuing you from the tavern and thus buying some time.*

Morgan came close to the house while seeking available cover. Just as Charlie showed him, he smudged out the tracks with a cedar limb from a nearby tree. At the same time, Morgan was aware of possible treachery from neighboring homes; one set of eyes was all it took. A report of the fugitives' whereabouts ... there was a bounty on his head. Fortunately, a window of the house was ajar. He hid in the shrubs while opening it wide enough to slip inside, looking carefully around before doing so. Success, he was in.

The house was quiet with only dim lighting muted through the closed curtains; yet Morgan could see it wasn't too neat. Morning dishes were left on the table, with the food hardly eaten. The house smelled clean enough, though. Morgan, on high alert, didn't know when the posse from the tavern would inevitably show up.

As for Charlie, he must have been hit, but Morgan couldn't think about that now. There were important instructions yet to follow. Hiding was the next step. Charlie had told him of a door under the floorboards that was covered by the couch in the living room. Sure enough, after moving the couch and rug, he found an almost invisible slide door; really a work of art.

Charlie told Morgan about this family secret during their trek through the mountains. Evidently, when the home was built, the cellar was intended as a cold storage area along with being a hideaway for runaway slaves. Great Grandpa was opposed to slavery, so he built the underground room to accommodate ten grown men. The room could be fully stocked with canned goods and survival necessities for a long time. Great Grandpa and his wife wanted to be assured the slaves survived. Charlie stumbled upon this hideaway one day when he was playing before being taken away by the authorities.

While Morgan was batting down the cobwebs in the cellar, the ground rumbled with the pounding of fast approaching horse hooves. The search party must have sent some guys back to check Mommy's house. Morgan quickly ducked into the underground hideaway, pulling the couch back over him and repositioning the carpet as best he could from below. Quickly he slid the trap door closed. The silence engulfed him. A perfect fit, Great Grandpa sure made it right. Once hidden, no slaves were retrieved from his house; the fugitives were lucky to find this refuge. Morgan huddled there, banking on that fact while thanking this long gone ancestor. Great Grandpa was connected with freedom fighters that helped to emancipate Negros. He was a hero then, and now beyond the grave, he was rescuing the life of his great grandson.

Bang, bang, bang at the door. "We know you're in there. Open this door before we kick it down." Out of the stillness inside, he heard soft slippers shuffling on the wood floor above his head. Heavy breathing and an uneven shuffle was the answer to the urgent demands from the uninvited guests waiting impatiently outside.

Click, click, as the bolts were turned, Mommy had lived a hard life alone all these years; she learned to keep safe from those who might take advantage of her. "Where is he, Melissa? Don't try to hide him from us! We'll find him if he's here," barked a gruff male voice.

Morgan heard his mother's confused response to the situation. "What are you boys so worked up about? I am on my deathbed and you guys come in here ranting and raving like a pack of wolves. What are you talking about?" she asked.

"Move, Melissa. We're searching this place for one of your boys," replied the man. At that the searchers breezed by the frail woman, leaving her muttering into the air.

There were heavy footsteps accompanied by the click of spurs on the wood floors above as Morgan cowered hardly breathing below. The men checked the house and attic thoroughly; their voices were filled with rage as they spit curses toward him and Mommy. Having ransacked the place, they were disappointed and stomped out their frustration because they left without their man.

Morgan waited what seemed like hours. Hearing a light tap on the floor above him, Mommy whispered, "Son, they're gone." At that he slid open the trap door, pushing away the carpet and couch to see his sweet little Mommy.

Helping him out of the hiding place, she embraced her son. He was just a little boy the last time they had seen one another, now he was almost thirteen. This was the moment he had dreamed about during all those hellish years they were separated.

His eyes stung as hot tears ran down his cheeks. Absorbed in this blessed reunion, his tiny mother was engulfed in her son's embrace. Years of loss and sorrow were overcome instantly by the healing power of love.

After a bit, they sat down holding hands and talked the remainder of the day well into the night. There was a lot to catch up on as mother and son asked unending questions of each other about their experiences over the years. As the story unfolded, there were both laughter and tears. Each listened intently to the other. Mommy fixed her long lost son a meal of toast, canned fruit, and hot tea from her bare kitchen, as Morgan brought out some dried meat from a recent catch.

That night, Morgan slept on the floor in his bedroll next to Mommy's bed. He was ready to flee at a moment's notice. There were too many things to set straight, and he couldn't allow himself to be captured. First, he must expose that drug house to the authorities so those helpless kids would be set free. He also had to explain why he and Charlie used the "borrowed" horses to ride home. Soon; but for now, exhausted he fell asleep.

Mid-afternoon next day he awoke to his mother's unsteady snoring. He quietly went to the kitchen to prepare a meal for them. Though the cupboards were practically bare, he discovered the underground cellar had plenty of canned goods that Mommy had gleaned from neighboring fruit trees and fields after harvest time. Morgan found an abundant supply of dried oats, barley, wheat, and corn, along with canned vegetables from her garden set aside for the day her children would return.

Mommy later told him what happened since he had been taken from her. This past year, having fallen sick, she had almost given up sobriety. Certainly not for lack of opportunity, yet she remained sober for both the kids and herself. She had to see them again. Though having lived recklessly, she didn't want to die that way. No, she was determined to end well, not leaving disgrace for her children to inherit. Though practically destitute, she somehow was able to pay the taxes on the family home. Her children wouldn't have to live on the street. She even gave up the money from dancing. Until a few months ago, she had been washing linen at the local hospital, but now hardly left the house, being so unsteady on her feet.

Pondering what she told him, Morgan heard a key turn in the front door. Before he knew it, he was practically face to face with Lydia, one of his mother's old running buddies, carrying two bags of food in her arms rather than the bottles and drugs of days gone by. She looked different, for a few teeth were missing and she was substantially heavier.

Setting the bags on the kitchen counter Lydia engulfed Morgan in her arms, then stepped back and peered at him through her thick glasses. "Which one are you?" she asked, smiling a nearly toothless grin. "You're so big and handsome, practically a man."

Mommy was out of bed making her pained entry. "I have to see if my son is truly here or if I was dreaming," she said. Watching from the kitchen door, tears of joy streamed down her cheeks, for her baby boy really was home!

Once Lydia saw her friend, she took the frail woman by the arm. Gently she helped her to a chair at the head of the table. Lydia proceeded to whip around the kitchen preparing coffee while heating the homemade meal she had brought. Morgan watched her and marveled at how graceful she was, considering her size.

After finishing their meal, though Mommy didn't eat much, they laughed and reminisced about the days when Mommy had all five kids with her. She had taken those days for granted. Not until recently did she realize that she was too absorbed with things that had choked the life out of them all.

Then came all the lonely years. Once the state took the children she was jolted into a war with her own demons. Attempting to get her children back, she had no idea of the battle ahead. It should have been easy, it seemed, but it wasn't. Rather, it was a vicious war with powers that be. Sissy was the first to be taken once word got out she had been abused. With her gone, the younger ones started wandering all over town looking for Mommy who was often absent. It wasn't long before the rest of the children were removed from her care.

At the beginning, there was a counselor who met with Mommy, attempting to help her make good life choices. Too soon, that woman was stricken with a deadly disease. At the beginning of the second year she died, and was replaced by a counselor disgusted with the system. For years prior to meeting Mommy the woman attempted to help others. But between the many abuses by parents, coupled with flaws in the legal system, by the time Mommy showed up, she was through trying to make a difference.

There had been a few victories, promises the girls would soon return, but Mommy crashed on the rocks after losing the first counselor. The shaky support from the second burned-out counselor along with the past glory days beckoning were just too much for Mommy and she succumbed with little resistance.

Overwhelming was the shame afterwards and the new counselor gave up on her completely. Many times, in a foggy stupor, Mommy marched into the state office demanding justice, demanding her children be returned to her. The employees just looked at her and laughed at the funny woman, but that didn't discourage her.

One fateful visit when she walked into the state office, one of the secretaries held up a mirror to her. The woman said she couldn't continue watching Mommy being beaten down like that. The face looking back in the mirror woke her up to the fact that between the damage done by her own lifestyle and the cruel treatment of those hired to supposedly help, it was time to end the torment.

Mommy had to confront the harsh truth about herself regardless if there was word about her children or not. Into the third year of their absence, she started attending recovery gatherings at the local church. Though not sober right away, she frequently attended. The church members and their Shepherd prayed for her as well as others in similar circumstances. Many of the townsfolk were in trouble, but with encouragement, some determined to get their life right. As for Mommy, once she got sober, she stayed sober. Visits to the authorities were now accompanied by the Shepherd, who stepped in to help get her children back.

Recently, Mommy started receiving letters from her daughters. They had begun supervised visits until she became too weak to see them. As for the boys, the authorities said they were settled, doing well in school. Charlie was in City College, living a happy, balanced life. As for Morgan, growing up without his mother had been difficult. They advised her not to disrupt the good in their lives by trying to get involved. "Think about how it would be if you deserted your sons again because of your illness," one woman said.

But of course she couldn't turn her back on them! She was their mother and wanted her children with her. Then she started getting sick, and with the accompanying confusion she backed off trying to reunite with the boys.

When Morgan and Charlie ran away from the boys' home, Mommy's friends told her immediately about the reward posted everywhere for their capture. Despite her health, this news strengthened her resolve to confront the system that held her children captive. With a poster of her boys in hand, she marched in and pounded her skinny little fist on the desk of her counselor. "If your foster home is better than my home, then why are my boys running away?" she demanded.

The Shepherd, members of the church, and her recovery group accompanied her. She was to be reckoned with now. Waiting unflinchingly, they stood and watched those previous tormentors stumble over excuses attempting to respond. They had no answers for what was happening.

"I want a full investigation, and I'm going to get one even if it's the last thing I do on earth," she warned.

Filling out complaint forms, she requested a hearing in front of the judge. What was going on in that "safe house" according to the state, that caused her "well-adjusted boys" to run away and become wanted men? The hearing was scheduled in a couple weeks, she revealed to Morgan.

Lydia noticed Mommy had become pale bringing up these issues and insisted she rest. Mommy's hands shook as she went into her room to lie down. Lydia tucked her in bed then joined Morgan in the living room, where she told him the details of Mommy's condition.She has seen numerous doctors and had many tests, but there is no remedy. "I do my best to keep her comfortable, but her condition won't improve," Lydia sighed. There was only a little time left. Possibly a couple months, they weren't sure.

Lydia had been coming over daily to care for Mommy since she became ill to feed and help her however she could. It was this last week since the big confrontation at the child welfare office, Mommy had become noticeably weaker. "I'm glad you're here and I know she is, too," Lydia said.

A knock at the door caused Morgan to scramble into the cellar through the door under the couch. It was the search party from yesterday. Lydia waited until he was safely hidden before opening the front door. They attempted to push their way in, but Lydia, like a huge mother bear protecting her cub, warned them if they so much as woke Melissa, she would personally discipline each of them. They knew she wasn't kidding and didn't want to get her upset, for her ways were well known. Very quietly, they snooped through the whole house, checking everywhere for Morgan. Lydia had cleared the table and put their dishes away while Morgan and Mommy were talking earlier. As for evidence of Morgan's overnight stay, it was hidden in the cellar.

The men left, unsuccessful yet again. Morgan was about to come from his hiding place when there was another knock on the door. Lydia answered. It was nosy neighbors that she didn't let in. Soon afterward another knock, from a couple church folks bringing fresh baked goods, but Lydia didn't let them in, either. Mommy wasn't up to visitors. When the house was finally still, Mommy woke and made her way to the living room. Lydia tapped the all clear on the cellar door to tell Morgan it was safe to come up.

The three of them realized the need to put together a plan to keep Morgan from the public eye. There must be no evidence of him in the house. Mommy wanted him to sleep in the cellar for his protection, but he insisted staying next to her in his bedroll. He promised to throw it down the cellar daily, erasing every step he made. The search party or anyone else could come snooping around anytime but would not be able to find him.

Once they established their plan for his well-being, Mommy looked directly at him and asked, "Son, tell us about the last six years. I want to know everything about that place and what you and your brothers have been doing." Leaning back, she waited.

Everything? He pondered the depth of meaning behind her question, recognizing in front of him was Mommy and her close friend. Though tough to talk about, revealing the truth to rescue those innocent kids was worth it for the facts must be told. There were parts he would prefer Mommy not hear, but she must.

Taking a deep breath, he started at the beginning. It was quite late when he finished. He spoke about her eldest, Teddy, who was still on the streets. He described all the horror they had endured, but when he got to the part about Charlie, all he could do was sob. No words as together they cried until they could weep no more. When Lydia left, Mommy and Morgan, exhausted, fell into a deep sleep.

True to his word, Morgan rolled up his bedding each morning and tossed it into the cellar, careful to leave no trace of being in the house. At first were frequent surprise visits from some good intentioned folks, but most were looking for the fugitive. Unsuccessful in finding Morgan, they eventually lost interest. Besides, they were looking for reward money, not a dying old woman.

Morgan and Mommy had a routine in the madness. Though there were doctor appointments, she didn't go because she knew her time was short and getting to those unnecessary visits would be a waste. The Shepherd visited regularly to encourage her, along with faithful Lydia, who was like a steady fixture around the place. Morgan hid in the cellar listening to every word spoken by the Shepherd. He had known plenty of evil people over his short life but could tell the Shepherd was truly a goodhearted man as he listened in to their chats.

Only Lydia and Mommy knew Morgan was there. Being confined to the house, they made the best of it. Fun times were woven into the midst of the challenges they faced. Lydia eventually moved in to help with Mommy's growing needs; it only made sense.

They started giving Morgan lessons to teach him some of the things he had missed while in the boys' home. Morgan's favorite was a trivia game about world events, history, and people. Filled with facts, Lydia and Mommy educated Morgan with stories from their families along with accounts of town history where they grew up, which fascinated Morgan, having missed these opportunities himself. They shared their knowledge from a number of topics learned over their lifetime, including what they knew about the origin of the human race from various perspectives. They did not want Morgan to fall behind his peers, so they home schooled him.

Using available books while drawing from their experiences, they focused on enriching his mind, soul, and spirit through family pictures, history books, and bedtime stories to recapture days gone by. They talked about science, math, plants, animals, human behavior, and, of course, Mommy's Holy Book. Mommy was good at connecting then and now, which made learning these subjects so interesting.

Chapter 5
Mommy Goes Home

Morgan, Mommy's treasured son, brought joy to her heart. She was thankful he was there, constantly available to care for her slightest need. Frequently during the night, she would awaken in pain, needing to be carried from one room to the next, which he gladly did.

Her body was breaking down. She prayed for the right timing, and her son's willingness to speak with the Shepherd about the eternity she would soon enter. There was no time for meaningless disagreements; instead, she was intent on savoring every moment together.

After much reflection, Mommy approached Morgan about the topic. She soon had to cross that bridge separating them on earth and wanted Morgan to someday join her. Feeling both sorrow and concern, not in going home, but that her son would be left alone again she was ready, for the King had prepared her.

Once she was gone, she told Morgan he must leave, too, for his purpose in this place would be over. She had challenged the institution that criminalized her family to the best of her ability, going as far as her body allowed. Radical changes would occur, but not in her lifetime. Morgan would have to take on that battle in the future. Mommy's role was to lay a solid foundation for him to live out his full potential according to the King's promise.

The time had come, soon the Shepherd would arrive. Sitting in the family room, she said, "Son, I have some important things to tell you, please listen closely." Mommy spoke of the past and her beloved children up until the present, then into their future as a family. She told him she was looking forward to seeing her own mother and father, and Charlie too. How would they look? When they were living, her parents attempted to tell her of the King, but she was too defiant back then. Her motto was her way, or hit the highway.

Not one to live in regrets, she knew her choices had cost much more than could be calculated. The price was not only her children, but lost opportunities to bring the King glory in speaking his message of hope. It grieved her heart as well as the King's, yet thankfully she returned to Him. Preparing to go to her eternal home brought Mommy much joy, with some sorrow because of the loved ones she must leave behind. Morgan sensed her loss as she reminded him one day they would be together— without the broken pieces. That was her vision of the future. "I'm ready to be with my own parents," Mommy said. "I sense their presence even now. Promise you won't rush through your days, for you have your whole life ahead of you. Live well, be well and cherish today, every day."

Mommy had written everything she could think of in a book to her children to help strengthen them during future trials. Her mother's heart was poured out on each page, including love notes to yet unborn grandchildren. Mommy gave Morgan the book she labored on over the years as part of her life journey from birth into eternity, to be kept by Morgan as a great treasure to share with the family. She wanted him to speak with the Shepherd, too. A trustworthy man, Mommy wanted Morgan to hear from his perspective what a privilege it was to know and serve the King.

Mommy asked Morgan to kneel by her so she could give a blessing from heaven to her son on earth. The connection was powerful! While they soaked in the beauty of this peace, there was a knock at the door. Lydia answered and let the Shepherd in.

While Mommy prayed for Morgan, Lydia prepared supper, which was now hot and ready to be served. Lydia ushered them all into the kitchen after brief introductions were made. The Shepherd appeared puzzled as he looked at Morgan, the missing son.

Together they enjoyed the hearty home cooked meal prepared by Lydia's loving hands. "You are an excellent cook," the Shepherd told her, making her smile.

After the meal, they shared laughter and news from town. Mommy requested the Shepherd repeat the morning sermon. After praying, he opened the Holy Book to reveal how the Word related to present day events. He spoke of Elijah, whose story is in the book of 1

Kings Chapter 16 to 19. How did this servant of the heavenly King deal with threats of destruction yet still rescue a nation from false belief?

"Read it, for this is what faces all who confront world systems. We must follow the Chief Shepherd. He alone will lead us in the right way to go," the Shepherd admonished them, while looking intently at Morgan.

The truths of the Holy Word pierced Morgan's heart, just as Charlie had when he spoke about the King. Morgan freely asked questions of the Shepherd about his complicated situation, for he felt safe with this man.

Late into the night they spoke. Concern about the future was wiped away from Morgan's mind as though it never was. "If our heavenly King can do this for Elijah, than He can for me," said Morgan. "I want this King as my King, reigning victorious." Everyone worshipped the King who alone deserves glory, honor and praise. Eternity belongs to Him. Confidently, Morgan committed every detail into His capable hands.

Filled with rejoicing, Mommy said, "When I am gone, get my boy safely to the sea. He has important business in faraway lands, for the King has called him there. There shall be many obstacles to overcome and lessons to be learned, but remember Elijah, my beloved child, and tonight. Draw strength on His truth aware that though we are not with you physically, we are shouting out *victory* in the name of our King. Press on! You are more than a conqueror through Him who loves you.[3] He can be trusted and will take you all the way."

Linking arms, the four gave a victory shout. Mommy mustered all her strength for this momentous occasion, and it showed. Immediately Lydia helped Mommy to bed. They knew these moments were their last ones together on earth. A few hours later, Mommy drew her final breath. Grief was present, yet so was the King as sweet peace enveloped them. Though there were tears, Morgan was grateful

---

3   Romans 8:37-39.

Mommy and Charlie were free and rejoicing with the King. No more pain, abuse, sorrow or fear; only joy, joy, joy.

It had been a privilege spending the last few months with Mommy. Morgan would miss her tender love, warm smile, and eyes that danced with childlike wonder to the end.

Now that Mommy and Charlie were gone, the events of the last few months began to catch up with Morgan. He was completely alone where it was too dangerous to connect with anyone, even his siblings. *What will I do? I'm only thirteen years old.* He began to heave deep sobs.

Part II
Adventures at Sea

Chapter 6
Mr. Millard's Businesses

All journeys have secret destinations of which the traveler is unaware.
—Martin Buber

Morgan was sad, but free. He furtively shuffled from Mommy's basement hideout to the Shepherd's house to be kept safe as long as possible. They said Morgan was the Shepherd's sister's kid and spent his days doing odd jobs for needy townspeople and members of the King's fellowship. Over dinner the family read stories from the Holy Book and communed with the King. In the short time since Mommy had passed, Morgan came to admire this family who made room to share their life with him.

Doing his best to change his appearance, Morgan soon realized it was too dangerous for him to keep hiding there, for people began making inquiries. What if the thugs looking for him found out he was there? As much as the Shepherd's family treated Morgan as their own child, he must move on. Recalling his mother's dying words, the sea was where he could disappear, grow up and stay anonymous.

Morgan heard about a firm called West Coast Shipping whose captain didn't ask many questions, so Morgan packed his few belongings, the journal from Mommy along with the Holy Book, and prepared to leave the next day. That night he thanked the family again for their love toward him. Not wanting to ask the Shepherd for help out of concern it might cause trouble, he decided he must let the family know about his plans. He was done sneaking around all the time, losing the people he loved.

Telling them actually went better than he thought. This Shepherd, like a kind father, understood how difficult it was for Morgan to miss the joy of family life, but because of the circumstances, he must leave into the unknown.

The Shepherd took Morgan to the docks—"It's best if I take you, less questions that way," he insisted. Dawn the next morning they loaded firewood into the wagon to not draw any attention, put Morgan's small bag under a few logs, and off they went.

As they traveled, the Shepherd recited from the Holy Book. He spoke about the cross and how the King had redeemed mankind. The Shepherd said, "We are bought and paid for at the price of our Creator's blood. Each of us is of tremendous value to Him. He delights to deliver us and takes great pleasure being in relationship with us.

"Wherever He leads, be in constant communion with Him and get close to His people. This will cause you to be effective all your days. There shall be many you meet who know nothing of Him. That is when you draw on what He has given you to tell them, for His heart yearns for the backslider. You have been through much, but there are even greater challenges ahead. Follow close to the King. His Word and His people will keep your soul sweet. Talk to Him about everything, do what He says, and try to keep it simple. No matter what comes, follow Him only." These comforting words spoken to Morgan helped equip him for the upcoming journey.

Before long they arrived at the shipyard. Upon entering the office, the Shepherd spoke briefly to the clerk who gave Morgan some papers to fill out. After checking his teeth, strength and reflexes he said, "The boy will do."

The Shepherd went over to Morgan, held him close, and said, "I would love to raise you as my own son, but that is not the path we shall trod, for you have a unique destiny apart from me. Things may appear good if you were to stay but instead you must travel on with the King, who is your perfect Father and knows what is best for you. Remember, there will always be room for you in my home as long as I live. I plan to change the situation at the boy's home and one day it shall be safe for you to return." Saying goodbye was not easy but those words assured Morgan he was loved very much.

The waiting ship had to be loaded and Morgan was sent immediately to work with the crew who stood side by side, passing crates from the dock to the ship. It was a dirty, sweaty job, this human assembly line. At mid-morning, the office clerk rang the break bell.

The men sat on the ground in the crisp spring air watching as a wagon from the fancy West Coast Hotel pull up. On the side of the carriage were painted the words, "Electric lights and steam heat, our hock meets all boats and trains." Not for common folk, they knew—just the wealthy could afford luxuries such as those demanded by the illustrious guests coming their way.

The door of the carriage opened and five men stepped out and went directly into the ship's office. The man in charge walked a leopard on a thick chain leash. Known as "Mr. Millard," he stood impatiently with cigar in hand as one of his guys hurried to light it for him. As the group walked past the resting crew, it was clear Mr. Millard was highly respected. Though a clear spring day, to Morgan it seemed an ominous cloud had appeared, and there was nothing he could do about it.

The break was almost over as the crew watched the men and leopard board the vessel. The clerk approached Morgan and tapped him on the shoulder. Taking him to a back room in the warehouse, he instructed Morgan to wash up and put on the clean uniform he was given. "When you're ready, report to the Captain," he ordered.

The *Iron Mistress* was a passenger freighter that was missing the Chief Steward's assistant. The captain of the vessel had observed Morgan handling his assigned tasks while loading the ship. He selected Morgan as his cabin boy and steward's assistant. "You're young, strong and healthy," he said to Morgan, "necessary assets for the job."

Morgan boarded the vessel, clean and smart in his new uniform and met the Chief Steward, who gave him the following instructions, "Don't ask questions, and just do as you are told." "Old Steward," as he was called, then showed Morgan around the ship adding several instructions regarding his upcoming duties.

Mr. Millard's party was to be Morgan's responsibility. They were already requesting a tub of warm water be drawn for the leopard's bath. Once the beast was cleaned up, he was to be fed some raw deer meat from cold storage below.

The ship had since cast off and was well under way, following the inland coast to open sea while Morgan attended to his duties.

Morgan's first chance to catch his breath after tending to the wild animal was interrupted by Old Steward. Cap'n Jack requested Morgan's attention as soon as he was through with the guests. With no time for a break, Morgan followed Old Steward to Cap'n Jack's quarters.

Old Steward gave detailed instructions to the new recruit, reminding him, "Be quiet, do as you are told, and all will go well. He is a busy man who doesn't like to be bothered. Set out the Captain's items nightly and have his steaming hot coffee delivered at 4:00 a.m. promptly. He goes topside at 4:40 a.m., and when he does, return and clean his room. The Captain expects order and excellence in your service to him. Once you are done, the remainder of your time is to be spent looking after the guests. 'Yes, sir; no, sir,' you are a non-entity, like a fly on the wall. If you have any questions, ask me, don't be a bother to anyone else. Am I clear?" asked Old Steward.

"Yes, sir," replied Morgan.

Morgan's days were spent caring for the Captain along with the many requests of the guests, and he soon entered a steady rhythm. He didn't have much time to think about personal needs such as sleep or food. He did everything while having continual communion with the King. Morgan saved all conversation for Him.

Morgan had been well schooled at that boy's home on being alert while remaining unnoticed. He alternated between feeding the snarling leopard and caring for the men's private quarters, along with looking after Cap'n Jack, of course. Mr. Millard demanded his bar remain stocked with drinks and appetizers for the ongoing party that started mid-afternoon daily.

Morgan was regarded as their servant and usually ignored. As a result he overheard juicy tales of wine, women, and song along with whispers of poaching, slaves, and drug trade. Their skilled business hands would grasp and take whatever awaited them upon reaching their destination. Morgan wondered what would happen once they arrived there. Since conditions were favorable with the wind and waves, they would soon arrive

In process of serving this rough bunch, Morgan heard details he preferred not to. Life to them had little significance, and a lowly cabin boy could easily be forgotten. Morgan made it his business to remain unimportant, never looking anyone in the eye. Instead, he fixed his gaze on the floor. He only spoke when spoken to and then simply in regard to orders. Proving reliable, he found the Millard party calling on him often, becoming even more loose-lipped in his presence. "Get this, do that," they insisted. The list seemed endless.

During the continual poker games, the guys really let down their guard. Vast amounts of cash flowed like water among them while they played. By now, they had become comfortable around Morgan, the man for the job. This group often hired the *Iron Mistress*. Since Mr. Millard employed part of the ship's crew exclusively for his private international business, things looked pretty good for Morgan.

Morgan was amazed at the vastness of the sea. Though most of his time was spent working, he sometimes went topside to breathe the invigorating ocean air. Feeling the wind and saltwater slap against his face was refreshing. As the weeks passed, Morgan became brawny and rough, growing to both fear and love the sea. He escaped any major storms like those he heard about the sea's raw power. His experience riding the wild waves was brief, and being jostled around reminded him of his recent cross-country trek on horseback. At times the waves became so choppy they were like a bucking bronco, and he was grateful for a wise Captain, sound vessel and caring King to keep all aboard safe.

The ship would soon arrive at port in the commercial center of Asia. Morgan was told her throbbing heartbeat could practically be felt. They would unload the ship and deposit her goods from the West, then reload with items of a much different nature. Evidently, poor families sold their children to anyone who would take them from the suffocating poverty.

Mr. Millard's men went to those struggling families with promises of a happy life beyond imagination that awaited the young beauties in the Land of Hope. A rich husband for the young pliable bride; for the boys, work in fancy homes wearing the best clothes while being fed every day. There were suggestions the child's benefactor might send for the whole family to rescue them from their plight.

Upon hearing such possibilities, the dads' eyes would sparkle a little. Maybe the whole family will receive a ticket to freedom. We'll wait out the winter until Mr. Millard's men return to buy the children—one here, one there. They were quite well paid for, though not always with money. All too often the exchange was drugs.

Mr. Millard's business thrived because his employees in Asia continually checked up on it. From farmer to peddler Mr. Millard had strongholds not only in Asia, but in other countries as well. His workers were loyal and did as they were told, for Mr. Millard was a hard taskmaster. Since many in his organization were customers; he also made sure they weren't crooked. Hence, his boys were his just like the leopard; wild, rough, even deadly, if need be.

Upon arriving, the *Iron Mistress* docked for a week. The crew gathered supplies to return across the Pacific while Mr. Millard and his men fanned out checking on the business. Two by two they went, demanding to see the farms and the books. The harvest had already been refined and was ready, waiting for Mr. Millard's arrival to ship out West. Usually farms and their shipments were in order.

This time, though, the authorities were after one of their best guys. A street urchin that worked his way up the ranks had recently become sloppy and was being followed. He had to be eliminated, messy work indeed. Deserted by his parents at a young age, he found success in distributing "product" to others on the streets. Recently using greater amounts, he was making a bad name for himself becoming wild-eyed and jumpy along with making late payments.

The Asian operation wanted Mr. Millard to tell them what to do, knowing if things weren't done the boss's way, they would end up as pig fodder. When he heard about the kid, he raged with anger and quickly gave his OK to have the kid eliminated, roughing up the leaders for not having done so already. He couldn't afford trouble. Drones like the boy were easy to come by. Unfortunately, this one had been a reliable producer with some potential.

Mr. Millard cranked up the wheels of the operation, getting everyone in line; keep the street setup quiet for a bit and focus instead on the shipment and moving the kids out West. Mr. Millard would soon leave his men to carry out his instructions, for they knew how he wanted things done; he never got involved with messy jobs like this. His role was giving orders, which he did very well. He was referred to by his Asian workers as "the Mist." Whenever the authorities got too close, he'd have someone pay them off—if they wouldn't accept the payment, poof! He erased everything, and everyone, that pointed back to him. You couldn't say he wasn't thorough.

Chuck Millard was a craftsman who got his orders from the Game Master. He wasn't interested in getting high off product; his pleasure was power. Being in the game with the Prince of Darkness gave him the shakes of ecstasy. Having the business running sweet and smooth, with plentiful money and gorgeous women embracing him, that was his thing. The edge of danger added delicious delight to the whole mix. Mr. Millard thrived when the show danced around him; some people were in terror being in his presence, and others mesmerized within his grip. That was his hit. At the peak of his game, he loved things hot and steamy. Once this little "Asia" problem was eliminated, everything would be just fine.

Mr. Millard had started out as a street kid in the icy north where he was born. The rush from deals made in illegal trade was his high. He tried the stuff but his dreams of being wealthy far outweighed the sick, out of control jolt he got from any drug. His mentor took Chuck under his wing, recognizing he had the makings of a tough business tycoon. "You're a real operator, kid," he told Chuck. He didn't know how correct that title was. Soon learning how the business was run, Chuck decided it was time to take it over.

At one of the sumptuous parties at his boss's place, Chuck Millard signed his soul over to the Game Master for foolproof plans to success. Everyone who was anyone in the business was there. Dinner was over and they were into serious drinking by then. His boss had a cigar casually hanging out of his mouth while the workers partied in the many rooms of the mansion with girl toys. Not Millard. He was hangin' with the high rollers, both enemies and associates. The boss lifted his whiskey in high spirits giving a toast, while everyone tipped their drinks to the business and young, up-and-coming Chuck.

That's when second-in-command Chuck Millard took out his pistol and shot his boss right between the eyes. The Game Master had coordinated it beautifully for there were no bodyguards around. Everyone drew their weapons, but shoot who, Chuck? Chuck Millard walked over to his dead boss, kicked his bloody body aside and ordered the wait staff to clean up announcing, "I'm boss now."

Surely an audacious move anyone less commanding would have been killed for, but not Chuck. After a moment, the drug lords shrugged their shoulders, lowered their weapons, lit up their cigars and patted Chuck on the back, welcoming him as the new CEO of the operation. The party went on as though nothing had happened and Chuck "inherited" everything: mansion, helpers, business, even his boss's voluptuous woman. He had the wife and kids eliminated though, collecting the life insurance. They were casualties; besides, he hated nagging women. Doing a clean takeover, he couldn't have the kids grow up to threaten business in the future. Oh, how he loved that sense of power throbbing through his body; Millard's idea of a perfect day.

He received instant authority. Though taking the business by storm, he didn't get everything overnight but calculated what to do next. Sometimes he went through "those" neighborhoods with all the mansions, looking for a toe in. Calculating and cruel, he never let anyone know who he really was. That is how he became such a trusted worker and powerful tycoon, by wearing the mask of a son but possessing the heart of a killer.

From the day he took over the lucrative drug trade in frigid Russia, he expanded it to the land of the East. Chuck Millard recognized her seething raw wealth was like a high-minded woman begging to be ravaged. "Asia."

Chapter 7
Asia, Land of Mystery

Asia ... a whispered word as soft as the Pacific breezes, yet mysterious as an unopened gift, exciting as the unexpected, a place Morgan quickly grew to love. Curving along the Pacific Rim, islands of exotic names flowing like the silks of Thailand, Bangkok, Penang, Kuala Lumpur, Singapore, Bali, rich in color and texture. How those names glide off the tongue, recalling fragrances so sweet they lull you to sleep and odors so harsh and raw they grab at your throat. The spewing millions of Hong Kong, Kowloon, wall-to-wall people. Rice paddies stair-stepping up the hillsides like giant water lily pads, emerald green with tender new shoots, the lifeblood of all eating. Exquisite gold leafed Buddhas, huge, ponderous, fierce Buddhas, soft, squatting, benign Buddhas. Temples and temple bells, some tinkling in delicate harmony, others booming in tomb-like reverberation. Exotic flowers in a fairyland of colors, strange, unfamiliar fruits of foreign tastes, textures, and aromas. Atolls surrounding islands, coral-making placid beaches, turquoise waters filled with darting fishes and ethereal shells. Mango and palm trees, oleander and hibiscus, bordering the golden sands to the sea.

The crowded Kalongs of Bangkok. Long, slender dugout boats, piled with a rainbow of flowers, vegetables, and fruit. Bloody raw meat, animal parts heaped in the middle of boats, drawing flies, begetting maggots. Open houses built on stilts over thick brown water. A bloated dead dog bobbing in the backwash of passing boats, the waves rolling it under a house.

Bali. Tranquility, gentleness, peace, the opposite of Hong Kong. Shy, golden brown people, graceful heads held erect, carrying piled offerings of fruit, beautifully decorated with woven grasses for the harvest festival. Their monkey dance, garbed in black and white checkered fabrics followed with the boisterous foot stamping and hand clapping ritual of masses honoring their beliefs. Singapore. The poor Raffles Hotel, growing smaller under layers of cracked, chipping paint, like an old dowager fighting age, filled with poignant memories of a golden past and its lost traditions of the old British Rule.

The Raj and its own mystic. Ghosts of English ladies and their gentlemen officers strolling garden pathways. The Singapore Sling, the high priest of all gin drinks. Pedi-cabs surrounding the curved driveway, a mélange of races waiting for a fare. Uncounted blending of all nationalities, all Asians. Asia, how it whispers. Asia ... Asia ... Asia.[4].

A ship's mate continued the story about Mr. Millard, the man who took what he wanted and left the rest. Dreams of treasure chests filled with gold and rare gems from these faraway places brought him only temporary excitement. His lust for wealth was comprised of an unquenchable desire for more, birthed from a heart that dwelled in the land of Never Enough. His lust for power ran hard and deep. He had built the business to include the Far East and Americas beyond frigid Russia, having farmed out that part of the operation.

As the ship's mate spoke, Morgan grasped this keen business sense was driven by the lust of the flesh, the lust of the eyes, and the pride of life. There was no drug or woman that could satisfy and though surrounded with great wealth gleaned from many nations, in his heart Mr. Millard was completely destitute.

The ship's mate said, "So that's the story of Chuck Millard, whose confusion started with a thought when he was a child. Both parents drank too much. Once his mom left, his dad was hardly home. When he showed up there were cruel words accompanied by harsh beatings, and I think that's why it was better when Chuck was alone."

Morgan thought about why Chuck turned to the life he led. He must have said, "I shouldn't have to live this way." The seed of resentment eventually birthed vast realms of "It's all about me." Rebellion and anger eventually turned into seething rage whose embers flamed

---

4   Lightly paraphrased from Liz Cohen, *Short Stories*. Used by permission.

quickly into a raging fire. By the time Chuck was ten he attempted to eke out his own way on the mean streets figuring it was better than the chaos of home. Morgan thought about Chuck and then himself. Unlike Morgan, Chuck had been unable to escape his childhood or the horrible things that happened there, and they helped form what he had become. Those experiences were seared into his memory, branding him forever as property of the Game Master. He was soon captured, paid in full without opportunity to even attempt escape. Chuck Millard runs the business but gets his cues from the Game Master, Morgan realized. It sure is amazing what a little thought can eventually become.

The ship's mate continued the story. "From the beginning he selected some men who used to work for his boss, of course training them so as not to allow what he got away with. They became trusted servants operating like a well-oiled machine. They respected his leadership, which was total control in every area. They knew their place, too. There were more men in the beginning, but their numbers dwindled for he had them killed if he distrusted them or they became too familiar with him. Chuck Millard left no room for error. Elusive and handsome, yet deadly, he knew how to handle people and get them to do what he wanted."

Morgan already knew there were tremendous consequences for this type of business, but Mr. Millard didn't seem to care about the depraved addicts, prostitutes, and broken lives left in the wake. Parents sold their children to him, and then lost their minds in a maze of condemnation. "A person can follow the trail of human wreckage to invariably find Chuck Millard," the ship's mate remarked.

For Morgan, being in the middle of such a dangerous operation was like jumping out of the frying pan into the fire. An orphan who had escaped one house of corruption now served a man whose little finger was greater in wickedness than the sum of all he yet knew.

Morgan cried out to the King, "What am I doing here?"

The King replied, "I understand your pain, but know my way shall bring a pain of its own. Giving up your wants and needs for Mine may seem bitter, but in the end it shall be sweet; whereas your way may seem sweet at the start, but the end is bitter. Take time to consider as you count the cost, My son."

Morgan would have to contemplate this proposition; what would happen if he agreed? Did he love the King more than even his own life? Still quite young, was he willing to be led by this unseen Force so many despised? Then he remembered Mommy, the Shepherd and the Words of life they spoke that made him brand new. It was a tremendous exchange, living a life of adventure with the King, versus Morgan doing his own thing. To give up all his whims, he definitely had to think about it.

He spent the first two days at dock preparing the cabins for the return guests, along with accompanying Old Steward to pick up supplies for the next voyage.

Chapter 8
Old Steward's Story

Old Steward needed Morgan's help, but that wasn't the only reason he told Morgan to join him that day. He saw something of value in the boy and wanted to teach the ways of ship trading and demonstrating how to haggle over purchases with the locals. Things were cheap, yet this tough old fella got them for less than half the asking price, which was no easy matter. He took the success of West Coast Shipping personally, telling Morgan the best years of his life were on board the *Iron Mistress* and how grateful he was for the job since everyone else had rejected him.

Old Steward told Morgan, "I was good as dead for the women and booze swept over me like a hurricane." He was a lot like Morgan when starting at sea. His mom died young and his dad was a violent drunk. Old Steward exchanged the chaos of land for peace he found at sea. He had weathered many storms, but still loved to ride the wild waves, a pleasure by comparison to home. On more than one occasion he rescued the ship, never tiring of its many challenges.

"Sadly, I also started drinking at a young age. One thing led to another and once I got married, our seven children followed in quick succession," he stated. What little time he got with them as a seafaring man was spent with a new baby or preparing for the next one. Periodically he spent time with his family but more often he chose the consuming life of alcohol in the arms of other women.

Did he quit the family, or did they quit him, he couldn't tell. The wife and kids finally divorced him for becoming a sloppy drunk, losing one job after another. He often ended up in a heap in strange places. Usually the ships' crew dumped him off with the cargo at the first stop.

Old Steward resigned to ending his life clasping his beloved bottle. But one day in a drunken stupor, a strange thing happened.

Slumped over on the sidewalk, he felt a gentle tap on the shoulder. Peering through bleary eyes, he saw a little girl gazing into his eyes while pointing to heaven. Before he could say anything, she disappeared as though she never was.

Immediately he was sober, but the most puzzling thing was desire for liquor had disappeared. Still smelly from a drunken jag, he entered the closest church. Though not knowing much about religion, he was desperate. Sitting down, he tried to put together the pieces of his life, how did he get here? Considering his childhood along with the wreckage of the past; his wife was a good woman. Why did he always walk away? What about the persistent call to the sea he loved? After a while he noticed how beautiful the church was, bringing a peace to his heart he had never experienced before. What was happening?

He left with many unanswered questions, got cleaned up, and went from one ship to another looking for a job. With his reputation ruined, no one would hire him. At his wit's end, he knocked on the door of the *Iron Mistress*. Cap'n Jack gave him a chance, which he didn't take for granted. That was almost twenty years ago and Old Steward was forever grateful. The first order of business was to reconcile with the wife and kids and though he tried, the family had lost all confidence in him. Just once they replied to his unending string of letters saying, "Leave us alone." Still, he never gave up hope. As for the job, he had worked his way from shoveling coal in the engine room to deck hand, then mess hall and now trusted steward.

The loss of his family was a continual reminder of an unattainable past, and one he could never regain. Only a miracle could bring them back and he believed in those. "Seen 'em many times at sea," he said. "Waves trenchin' so deep the trusty *Iron Mistress* seemed like a child's toy bouncing around, almost shattering."

He knew a few fellas over the years who gave credit for their safety to one called the King, but Old Steward wasn't convinced He even existed; besides, he had no time for tall fish tales. "But time has a way of softening a man," Old Steward commented.

He questioned that if this King supposedly cared so much for people and could do anything, why didn't He bring together his broken family? Now that his life had changed, he needed and wanted them. "Tell me why He can't fix this?" he asked. One of many questions no one seemed to be able to answer. He sure wasn't expecting this kid to say anything he hadn't already heard.

Morgan replied, "Actually today I plan on talking with Him regarding some requests of my own. I'll ask Him to visit you, and then you can talk to Him yourself." Morgan took these concerns seriously, having plenty of unanswered questions that he couldn't bear any more either.

Morgan's proposition completely stunned Old Steward; the elder man actually forgot he was there as they carried the supplies back to the ship. Upon reaching their destination, Old Steward stopped abruptly. Looking at Morgan he said, "Tonight, eight sharp. Tell Him I'll be expectin' Him."

Morgan replied, "All I can do is ask."

Old Steward dismissed Morgan, and then instructed a couple deck hands to put the supplies away. Morgan hung around long enough to get a bite to eat, and then retired to his shared cabin below.

He sat down on his bunk trying to still his racing mind. It had been days since their last conversation. When they spoke previously, the King requested that Morgan give up some things and he wanted to be ready. What it meant he didn't know. One thing for sure, it involved sacrificing personal desires.

After pondering how things had been, was he ready for this type of commitment? Since he had met the King, the problems hadn't gone away. They were different, yes—but there were still problems. He remembered his vulnerable past with loneliness as his constant companion, whereas with the King, he was never alone. What about the exquisite reunion with his brother and Mommy, meeting the Shepherd, and the joy of meeting the King the night Mommy went to heaven? He had become used to being shuffled around so he wouldn't be captured or killed. Now he was alone again with a bunch of strangers in a strange land, doing strange things.

He had nothing to offer but a sad and broken heart. He couldn't go back —besides, where was home? Anything was better than what his future held at this crossroads without the King in his life.

The King interrupted his meditations:

Beloved Child,
I have brought you here, far away from what you know, to speak with you about some things. The place you have been all your life is now too small for you. I have been preparing you since conception, even the foundations of the very earth, for this conversation. I have waited for you to ask for Me, and now I shall speak. As for the loss, the pain and abuse, even the death of those you love: All your dreams crashing to the ground have happened for a reason; to bring My purposes into your life. I want you to dig deep past your own understanding to the place I alone reside. Enter this place; come past the battles both real and imagined. Breathe Me into your heart and listen. Drink deeply from My mouth into your ears. I shall roll through your whole being to plant the desire of My heart, but only if you agree.

Terrified at his condition compared to the Holy One, he confessed all. His gleeful attitude of murderous revenge toward injustice and atrocities from one person to another; his difficult life as an orphan and fugitive; hatred for the people he had lived with at the boys' home; following Wisdom to the *Iron Mistress,* and the mess his soul was in. He said, "What a horrible attitude of heart, I know it's wrong. I keep bumping into myself while telling you about it, repenting and offering forgiveness to those who hurt me, then hating them all over again. This will not be over until you step in and change me from the inside out. Though I deserve your harsh judgment, instead I ask for power to overcome this curse in my flesh. You alone can change me, and I choose to agree with the process. Please have mercy on me and rescue me, in your name, Amen."
The King responded:

My beloved child,
You alone hold the key to your heart. If you give it to Me, I shall turn the key and unlock the treasure chest of life within you. Do you trust Me enough to give Me that key? It shall be easy, having opened your heart to me on other occasions, you understand. What I am ask-

ing is full ownership of your heart with the access to come and go as I desire. This means I will own your heart. No heart or blood disease shall touch you, instead all shall function normally. There will be a transition time though. Are you willing to be My love slave"?

At that, Morgan buckled. "What!" he cried. His whole life he had been someone's prisoner. He didn't want to be controlled by anyone ever again.

The King continued:

This is very different from what you think. My love and plans for you are perfect. This step of surrender is absolutely necessary before you can walk the way I have chosen. There is a hard path ahead. Prepare well for you are my holy instrument chosen to set many captives free, but not as you think. This is why you must give me total ownership of your heart. Will you trust Me here and now? Can you?

Over the last few days Morgan had thought quite a bit about who the King was to him. He pondered that question once more before saying:

You are all I have. I have no family, no name and no future, nothing except You. Everything I hold dear is gone. My heart key that I hold, I surrender joyfully and full of faith, for you alone are worthy of everything I possess. Until I met You, I was put into numerous degrading situations. I hoped for escape to experience love and healing with my family, instead further pain and loss occurred. This choice to give You the key to my heart I do sincerely with no shame attached. I have peace and give both the key and my heart to You only, for you are worthy.

Morgan then remembered a story the Shepherd had told him before departing his hometown:

"What lack I yet?" When the King answered the rich young ruler's question, the young man said: "All these rules have I kept:

what lack I yet?" Then the King revealed his lack and he went away sorrowful. When the interview was over; the King asked for the Key, but the young man refused to give it.

As Morgan willingly gave his days to the King, the words of the Shepherd rang in his head:

Does the King possess the keys to your life? Has He the key to the Library of your life, or do you just read what you please? Has He the key to the Dining-room of your life—do you feed your soul on His Word? Has He the key to the Recreation compartment, or do you just go where you please? Have you given the King the Master Key to your life?

We may have all of Wisdom, but has He all of us? Are there spaces yet to be filled with Wisdom—spaces, places, rooms and closets in our spiritual house into which He has not "fully come," because we have not yet given up all the keys, from cellar to attic of our spiritual homestead?[5]

Once Morgan finished his prayer the King spoke:

My beloved,

You belong to Me. Nothing withheld. I am your King. Be still and watch Me. Do as I show you. I love you. Enjoy your brand new life. I heard Old Steward's request and shall visit him tonight. He will tell you about it when he is ready.

The dinner bell rang, but Morgan was not interested in food. He had been fed a banquet already that completely satisfied and choose to remain at rest with his King. Delivered from needing to figure things out through his mind, he now trusted fully in the King. The rage in his heart was gone, filled with hope beyond grasping instead.

---

5   Mrs. Charles E. Cowan, *Springs in the Valley*, December 23, 350—have changed original "Jesus" to "the King" for the story line without changing meaning of the words.

Morgan knew everything was going to work out as he sank into a deep sleep.

Next morning he fixed Cap'n Jack's fire and coffee as usual. The Captain, who hardly uttered a word, used to annoy Morgan, but no more, for he accepted challenges better. Going about his duties, he noticed a new way of thinking.

Whenever things didn't make sense, Morgan now said, "The King knows what he is doing," or, "This is an opportunity for growth." Even memories of the painful past and concern for the troublesome future were lessened. Though not answering all his questions, that was no longer important because Morgan had a fresh sense of purpose. Even Mr. Millard and his gang returning aboard the vessel didn't trouble him.

Chapter 9
The Band of Brothers

While the ship was docked, Morgan got to know some of the other believers on board who met regularly with the King. This comforted him, bringing back good memories of Mommy and home. Familiar with his duties after the first voyage, Morgan discovered ways to meet topside after work.

Their time together was unique, waiting quiet and still before speaking. Morgan initially thought it was exhaustion, then realized they were waiting to commune with the King without interference. It is too easy to focus on others rather than Him. He is always present, and wants us to want Him rather than use control or manipulation to draw our affections toward Him.

There was great value in these evening gatherings, singing and reading from the Holy Word. Talking with Him brought clarity to the most baffling situations. The best part was no matter what, the King loved them, which caused Morgan to love Him even more.

The first night Morgan met with the group, a young guy was there who followed the King yet still flirted with the Game Master. Easily tricked, he would listen to whatever came his way. Unable to separate the truth from a lie, the young man ran with the Game Master until coming aboard the *Iron Mistress*. Someone invited him to these gatherings, where he had met the King a few weeks earlier.

This particular night, he had his head down. After a bit, he confessed to spending the last few days hanging out with the Game Master. Sure, he heard Wisdom calling him back, but pride wouldn't allow him to listen, and his heart was quickly becoming hard. Attempting to turn away from the excitement of the Game Master, he couldn't. He was stuck, with disaster looming ahead. The group gathered around him and talked with the King on his behalf. One of the men quoted from the Holy Book: "For though a righteous *man* falls seven times, he rises again."[6]

Deeply emotional, as they continued, another guy confessed to hiding some things; then another admitted to flirting with the Game Master too. As they confessed their faults to each other, the love and forgiveness was overpowering. Accountability grew as they revealed more secrets, thus causing greater appreciation for one another. The best part was the love and forgiveness they felt as the King spoke to each one. How could He be available to each of them at the same time? It was a great mystery.

Meeting regularly meant the band of brothers didn't struggle alone. Instead, they discovered their purpose in the journey as they overcame many obstacles together. As for the confused man, the next time they gathered he was totally changed, for he had escaped the trap set by the Game Master and now lived in peace.

The day before the *Iron Mistress's* departure west, there was a flurry of activity with all hands on deck. The passenger quarters had been thoroughly cleaned and sumptuously decorated. Old Steward made sure every detail was done to Mr. Millard's expectations. As a reliable customer who paid top dollar, he demanded excellence.

One crate after another was loaded in the lower bowels of the vessel and properly secured. Though the work had been going on all week, the last push was always a tumult of activity, besides, this season was better than most. This port already gathered the winter's goods into storage in preparation for export, so there was plenty to pack into the ship.

There were always loose ends to arrange and this time was no different. An elephant trainer was coming along with his elephant to transport across the Atlantic. The animal required a tremendous amount of space and sedatives. Morgan was to direct the children Mr. Millard brought on board to do the majority of caring for the animal. This was no small task. The kids on this return voyage weren't going to stay in first class, but were tended by a couple of Mr. Millard's people below.

6   Proverbs 24:16 (NIV)

The band of brothers was exhausted that night from speaking about these heavy issues with the King. Under the stars, they meditated quietly together. That is when Morgan brought the matter regarding his involvement with the kids to the King, who counseled, "Return." This puzzled Morgan. He had heard this before when he tried returning to Mommy and a normal family life. That didn't go as planned. Neither did giving his life to the King or letting go of cherished behaviors. What could this instruction of "Return" possibly mean? How can he return to something that doesn't exist? Morgan didn't want to be alone. What's more, his relationships were becoming healthy. Besides, what did returning have to do with the challenges he was facing? It surely couldn't apply to close ties with Mr. Millard and his group. By the end of the evening, though filled with peace regarding this next voyage, Morgan was no closer to understanding what the King meant.

Next morning after Morgan attended to Cap'n Jack, he went to check on Rhino the elephant. Morgan cleaned his pen, but the elephant's care was done by the trainer alone. There were strong sedatives to administer when they departed so the elephant would sleep calmly across the rough waters until they arrived at their destination; at least that is what they hoped.

Once everyone was aboard, Morgan would help with any of the passengers' needs. Though it was a busy day, Morgan continued to meditate upon the King's exhortation: "Return."

Chapter 10
Preparation

"Return" stuck like a lump in Morgan's limited understanding. Only the King could open his thinking to the truth. For every question, He always provides the answer as Morgan had learned. Since childhood Morgan had been prepared for a great purpose in the King's eternal kingdom. Though often painful, he recognized those experiences were helping to build a bridge to cross the great chasm between then and now.

The King is preparing me to be his warrior. Morgan was sure of that, but first his affiliations must be tested, for there was a great war on behalf of men's souls he must brave. He considered the teachings of the Shepherd regarding the battle.

The need is immense yet the battle is fierce. It began before man or creation. The King, Abba Father and Wisdom, referred to as the Trinity, created heavenly beings; great holy ones. There was a mighty administrator and most beloved friend of the Trinity whose name was Son of the Dawn. He would commune with the Trinity, ruling a third of the holy ones in the eternal city.

One day Son of the Dawn birthed pride, which sparked the rebellion that changed everything. The Trinity knew about this, yet allowed the rebellion to carry on. How the One of pure love must have felt is beyond comprehension. Why did they who possess all power allow it? Yet they did, and at the time appointed sent the betrayers down to the dark planet referred to as earth.

Was the nothing and chaos a result of this banishment, or was dark earth conceived in the mind of the Creator? Regardless, the Creator created earth and man. The human was the object of the Creator's love, precious to the Creator, who set him apart from all others by giving him free choice. Overwhelmingly, this gift of love meant that man may *choose* Him instead of being made exclusively to worship Him, as the betrayers had been fashioned.

Who would man choose? Would he love the Lover, or pursue the Betrayer? That was the whole point, the opportunity for the creature to triumph over rebellion. But that did not happen. Instead, the love gift of free choice produced confusion and deception in man and temptation ruled. The Betrayer tricked the created, encouraging them to rebel. The result, man and woman were removed from that perfect estate of being face to face with the Trinity, harsh consequences of heeding the lies of the Betrayer.

How could this happen? The Father of Lies succeeded over man's free will all too easily. Renamed Satan, the master of deception known also as the Game Master had won the prize of dominion he so coveted. As for the authority of man, the spoils were divided among the Game Master and his horde.

Overwhelming loss in the holy kingdom, yet the Trinity knew all along of the dreadful deceit buried within the heart of His creation. Now His creation, sullied from the treachery of sin, must be rescued. He attempted to speak to their good senses, but to no avail. That ancient deception with its tremendous power caused many to perish with no trouble in being led by that tricky Game Master. Trinity alone possessed the cure, but it required our choice, too.

The Game Master laughed in the Creator's face, taunting, "Look how easily this little mutton turns away and frolics with me!" There were promises of a Redeemer, but the Game Master successfully intercepted men's attempts to be free over the eons. Deceptions too powerful to combat seemed to rule them. For many generations the Game Master with his wicked hoard flourished while ruling over men and women who consistently chose folly over Wisdom.

But one day the Promised One arrived. A little baby was miraculously birthed by a virgin in a cave that served as a stable. "No room at an inn," they were told, let alone the palace of splendor where he should have been born; yet it was just as the Holy Book foretold. The Game Master and his followers immediately went into a panic. "Kill! Destroy!" they incited the humans. Though many lost their lives, it was to no avail, for the baby grew to manhood. Finally, the Betrayer lured a person dear to the Promised One to be disloyal to Him. A blood bath followed as the hordes of hell threw the victory party to top all of their greatest celebrations, for man's Redeemer bled to death on a cruel cross.

At the height of their rejoicing, a loud crack above was heard, ripping all into separation eternally. It seemed Abba Father had awakened like a Man of war robbed of His young. All creation shook to its core and became deadly dark that day. The keys to death, hell, and the grave in the bloody battle for souls were totally reclaimed by the One True God. "I Am King of kings and LORD of lords," He thundered. The moment so long awaited had arrived. He freed the captives who chose to follow Him.

The Game Master's realm was ransacked as one by one souls were led triumphantly out of darkness into the glorious light of the kingdom of the Son, our King. Authority no longer in his grasp, the Game Master could only pretend to possess the keys. Yet the Game Master still has the power to deceive, and is often successful.

The Trinity's design to buy back the souls of men by the blood of the King was one hundred percent victorious. His death, burial, resurrection and ascension paid for our eternal redemption. Morgan learned: Believing is the requirement of passage, that invisible passport defining the transition of man from the temporary state of confusion to the King's eternal home of glory. His redeemed creation was now washed and brand new—Morgan knew the whole truth, for it can be read by all from the Holy Book. Man was restored to perfection forever! The wicked hoard had evidently forgotten who they were dealing with.

The King spoke to Morgan during their intimate time, saying, "Morgan, I call all My beloved ones to return to Me. Not out of this life, but into My plan of original intent."

Finally Morgan understood, for the truth hit him: He wants us to know He loves us and created us to love Him and one other. But all too often we get confused along the way and though fashioned to love we're tricked to choose rebellion. Since we can't serve two masters, we end up hating the Creator, bringing separation, anger, and eventually death.

Morgan had been driven by a passion to be "normal," but once he realized he was created to lavish his love upon the King, that was all he desired. The uncertain future didn't seem to matter as much as before. "I choose You alone, O King," he shouted within.

Morgan was not confined to a meager allotment in life—no. Instead he was radically connected to the Source of all love and power, a Friend like no other. The fear and darkness vanished with this revelation. Though trials and storms would certainly come, they now held much less influence. Armed with this conviction, Morgan knew whatever lay ahead, he was forever free to be his created self.

In that moment something mysterious occurred to Morgan. He passed through the dark tunnel of the Game Master's oppression into the full light of the Trinity's kingdom. Not cocky in the least, he chose to humble himself through the process of transformation, fully aware of how far he had traveled. Far from the land of his birth, Morgan had returned home. What a marvelous Redeemer; the only One who could accomplish such a thing.

Jubilation filled his soul, causing Morgan to pause on deck briefly and collect his thoughts before the passengers boarded. To be invited to partner with the Redeemer and set souls free by battling as His warrior delighted him. Remembering his journey was not as painful now; rather it propelled him into action. Through the pain and loss, the Comforter had removed the poison from his heart. Morgan could now share this gift of comfort with others—not on merit, but because of the King. Very soon he would be called upon to engage in that war.

Morgan's thoughts were broken by a series of events that would translate those ideas into action. Watching the procession boarding the ship, he saw the group of young boys and girls that had been purchased by Mr. Millard's operation. They were making their way toward him through the crowded maze accompanied by Mr. Millard's men and one woman, Mr. Millard would arrive later.

The adults looked like duck parents waddling their ducklings to the lake, crossing a busy intersection. Other passengers approached as Morgan and Old Steward greeted them at the gangplank. Old Steward escorted the adults to their staterooms where the accommodations had already been prepared for their comfort, while Morgan walked the children and caretakers below. An idea occurred to Morgan— teach the children as Mommy and Lydia taught him back home. Not knowing how to accomplish this, Morgan believed that Wisdom would guide the way.

With so many pressing needs, it wasn't long before Morgan realized he was in over his head. These children were strangely quiet, seeming to sense their bleak future. Not knowing where they were, sad, scared or both, they spoke few words. It was odd they shed no tears, not even the little ones. Morgan couldn't stay long, for the Millard party had priority. When he returned, the children had unpacked their belongings and were in the playroom, though it didn't look much like play.

The three adults tending them were very efficient. Frank and Ted had served Mr. Millard since their teens. Well trusted, now in their mid-forties, they were like brothers united in the dangerous life they led. There was a secret language between them. During the previous voyage, Morgan noticed the lack of words yet perfectly coordinated actions. A look, a tap of a cigar, or a raised eyebrow spoke volumes for these two.

Betty was very different from the two men, with her steady stream of giggles and chatter. She was Frank's wife, quite young and beautiful indeed. She spoke with an accent and wore low cut tops and tight fitting bottoms to reveal that provocative figure of hers, fre- quently sashaying past Frank and Ted to tussle one of the children's hair. Everyone noticed when she bent low, for there was too much information given. The men looked, and then exchanged glances. Betty didn't seem too bright, but she sure was good with the kids. Pretty quickly Morgan summed up she was Frank's play toy.

Betty knew what others thought of her. It's obvious with their looks and hush-hush whispers behind my back. They don't know me, she thought to herself. They only see how I act. What they don't know is my hunger for someone, anyone, to wash away all the cruel deeds done to me during my childhood. I long for love and acceptance, but all I ever get is cruelty and rejection. I thought Frank would be different, but he is just a man like all the others who have used and abused me. I believe somewhere in his dark heart he loves and cares for me, but not anywhere near what I need.

Morgan let the passengers know he was at their service and whenever needed could be contacted via the ship's phone. Previously the adults told the children about Rhino and they were looking forward to see the elephant. Before going to his pen, Morgan asked the trainer to give clear instructions on caring for the enormous beast. The children were instructed they must be accompanied by an adult at all times because Rhino might get angry and harm them.

Though the elephant would be sedated the entire voyage, the trainer told the kids he didn't want any problems. Kids and elephants could be a bad mix fast if handled improperly, and any misfortune must be avoided at all cost. Once the children cleaned the pen and prepared the food, the trainer dismissed the crowd to administer the sedative. The drugs were powerful with tremendous street value, thus kept under lock and key all the time.

The kids always stayed as long as they could with the beast during the voyage. It was obvious they loved the gentle giant and he seemed to love them, too. They related well, as though they could identify with each other. Sharing the plight of being taken from all they knew, going into a future of uncertainty brought instant kinship. It was painful for Morgan to watch the adults usher the children from the animals' quarters knowing the comfort the elephant gave them. The power others had reminded him how helpless to stop the insanity of their plight he really was. All too often, protective instincts rose up as he felt himself being sucked into a vortex of uncontrollable emotions. Wisdom would then appear and hold him tight saying, "Stop the feelings before they start. Be still and know the King is in charge, even here in these impossible circumstances."As Morgan acted on these truths, the awful feelings would lessen.

While tending to his duties, Morgan made sure to reflect upon each child's name and pray for them. The only way to stay out of confusion over this heartbreaking situation was to run to the King who always knew what to do.

Morgan's heart became joined to the children, each so precious and perfect. How could he help them? Not yet an adult himself, he considered the options. Though wanting to throw those with wicked intent into the sea, he couldn't, nor could he parent each abused child. Besides, for each one here, there were untold thousands treated much worse. Here and now was his time to help these kids.

The workday closed late the first day, and that is when he gathered briefly with the band of brothers. They talked about the children, who were everyone's primary concern. These trips were always painful for the crew; that is for the ones who made room to care. The men cried out to the King. He responded by guiding them in a way far different than what they imagined.

"Focus on the adults," said the King. "They are the key. I want to intervene and change the direction of their lives. Not only will the outcome of these children be impacted, but many others shall be spared as a result. Your call is to pray and bless them."

Though challenging, that is just what they did while waiting on further instruction from the King for each person—Ted, Betty, Frank, Mr. Millard, Morgan—even including the elephant in their prayers. "What about the children?" Morgan asked.

The King responded, "That, too, shall be revealed in My time. For now, stay close to Me."

Chapter 11
Frank and Betty

As the group finished praying, one of the seasoned crew members took Morgan aside and recounted the history of Frank and Betty's seafaring adventures. This is what he said:

"As you know, Mr. Millard and most of his men are from up north. When I first started with Cap'n Jack aboard the *Iron Mistress*, everyone was much younger then. Those fellas all had dark hair, not even beards yet. Frank wasn't quite twenty according to my guess, married to another gal—can't seem to remember her name. It'll come to me … oh yeah, Posy, like the ring around the posy. She was something else. They all were back then. Fire hot, with a quick trigger finger—a real wildcat.

"Anyhow, Frank was kinda frisky around the youngsters, chargin' 'em like a wild stallion. As you could imagine, Posy didn't take too kindly to that, plus those were just little girls. You know how some gals are around grown men, and Frank was a looker back then, too. It was easy for him to breed with them. Well, this went on for a while. Posy used to do Betty's job, helping Frank and Ted and such.

"We were on an ordinary summer transport from the north where Mr. Millard is from; that's when Betty showed up, not even twelve. 'Little Miss Hot Stuff'—actually, I sympathize with her, being she was bought at a slave auction from some drunken pirates. Ted, Frank, and Posy settled into their duties, and of course, Frank took on extra ones with Betty. That's when the bumpy trip started. The way I see it, Betty didn't want to do any more of that drudgery, and probably thought if she could get in with Frankie boy, there would be no more of it.

"Frank and Betty often showed up top deck together to get alone, but that didn't go over well with Posy. She and Ted trudged along with that 'sorry lot of kids below' while her man played around with the young trollop. I know all this 'cause I caught glimpses while going about my duties. I was just a scalawag then, slopping mop buckets, low kid on the totem pole, but sure saw some interesting things.

"Well, back to the story. Posy would come topside to spy on Frank and Betty, biding her time, I suppose. One day she appears sly like, right up to 'em. Before they knew what happened, out comes a blade. She started swingin' it 'round like a sword, slashing and thrashing, attempting to cut the little lovebirds to ribbons. The reason I know is I heard the commotion from where I was moppin' and trotted toward 'em. Saw the tussle with Frank just as he sent Posy overboard into the drink.

"It was rough waves that day and before I could get the life ring, the sea swallowed her up. Frank pulled me up close and said if I squealed, I'd end up like a stuck pig. I am an orphan, you know. Don't have anyone in the world but me. I was scared to death, even peed my pants being I was barely a kid myself. Who would care about a lost kid at sea? So I kept quiet all these years and clammed up real good. Well, Frank made Betty and me help clean up the mess and throw all the evidence in the sea where Posy was already eaten by sharks or the like.

"Frank put together a fancy alibi saying Posy was seasick, pukin' up everywhere. Declared he and Betty brought her topside to get some air when she stumbled, hit her leg, and lost her balance. Over she went and with the help of the wild ride, the hungry waves ate her right up. Before they could save her, she disappeared from sight, end of story.

"No one pushed it. Even Mr. Millard felt sorry for that sneaky Frank, as he was slobbering and blubbering like a hungry baby seal for his missing mommy. Mr. Millard gave Betty to Frank as a gift to calm him down. Before this all happened, there was a point everyone thought Mr. Millard would kill Frank. Jumpin' those young'uns like Frank was doing was messing up the fancy import export business. This situation provided a perfect truce of sorts; Mr. Millard gave Betty to Frank and no more 'Mr. Frisky' with the kids. Frank owed Mr. Millard big for that secret. You see, everyone knew Frank killed

Posy, but Mr. Millard bullied us to accept the phony tale. Done deal, that's how Mr. Millard runs his stuff. If he owns 'em, he doesn't have to kill 'em when they cross the line, and Frank was his man, signed, sealed, and delivered.

"One more thing: I think Frank was crying like that in sheer terror of what Mr. Millard really might do. It couldn't have been sadness over the death of his wife. So Frank and Betty live happy ever after, sort of, while the kids are safe from Mr. Frisky. As for Ted, well, he's a strange duck-in a different world, let's see ya' try to figure that one out. Now you know how Mr. Millard keeps the details of his business exactly the way he wants 'em.

"A little warning, I think Betty is tired of Frank. All growed up, she's the frisky one now; and Frank, he's too old to keep her busy. You watch yourself 'cause she likes the young hard- working muscly crew. She knows how to get a man's attention, too. Remember: danger! Be sure to put that sign in big red letters every place she tries to flash you with her goodies. Don't let her get to ya 'cause then you'll have both Mr. Millard and Frank to contend with. You know what that means."

When the fellow finished his story, things made a lot more sense to Morgan. Since it was late, he returned to his bunk for a short rest. Four a.m. arrived faster than usual. Although groggy, he quickly got up to serve Cap'n Jack his coffee. Surprisingly, Cap'n Jack spoke to Morgan. "Don't think broken hearts are forever. Let the sunlight of the Spirit of love shine on those hurting and broken places. The King wants to heal every one. Feel His touch, then bring that healing to others."

This was the most Cap'n Jack had spoken to Morgan since starting work aboard the *Iron Mistress. Rather unusual, yet definitely a message from the King.*

"Do you know the King, sir?" Morgan asked.

"I did, long ago, but lost touch with Him," The Captain answered. "I'm not a big one for words, but I'll tell you this: I felt His hand on me often during my life, and have been hearing Him again recently. It is obvious you know Him, which has affected me for good. Actually, last night He came to visit my cabin and I renewed my relationship with Him in a way that never was before—a long time in coming, I suppose. Anyhow, He told me to look after you, for He is preparing you for something real special." The Captain then laid his hand on Morgan's heart, and prayed for the boy.

Filled with strength, these words and actions were as healing oil poured over Morgan's confused heart. He asked himself, "Aren't we all in dire need of the King's love? I know I but perish without Him."

Morgan celebrated a heavenly festival, while choosing to enter the next place the King had prepared. When the King calls many refuse, although some do say yes. Morgan breathed in deeply His call; moving into the day, he savored the Living Water that engulfed him.

Chapter 12
New Followers of the King

Overflowing with Wisdom's presence and empowered by the King's love, Morgan approached Mr. Millard's quarters freshly equipped as the servant of the Most High. His role was to trust what came next would be as the King wanted. Being able to speak on behalf of the King when given opportunity was part of the blessing he received from Cap'n Jack.

On the surface, everything remained the same as Morgan gathered soiled laundry and dirty dishes from the servant's cabinet outside Mr. Millard's cabin door. The real work was not these menial tasks, but from the inside, every breath a prayer. "Get their attention," Morgan cried within his heart while doing his duties. Whether he washed clothes or comforted an upset child, Morgan knew the King was there, certain that whatever he asked, the King would answer.

At one point, Mr. Millard and his gang called Morgan into their quarters, pressing him with questions. "You're different from other guys," one of them said.

"Yeah, we're curious," added another. "How can we have authority like you without manipulating others?" Bored with the poker game, they invited Morgan to sit down and tell them the source of this gift. Knowing they were headed down a dead end, they wanted the serenity Morgan demonstrated. As for Mr. Millard, he didn't ask questions, but listened to what Morgan had to say.

Morgan not only spoke truth from the Holy Book, he related his intimate relationship with the King. It seemed Frank, Tom and Betty along with Mr. Millard's men were intrigued, yet struggled with accepting the King. What would He require of them? What kind of a Ruler was He? Could they trust Him to do as He promised? These were some questions they needed answers to. Daily they pressed

Morgan to tell them more about this One who seemed so different from the Game Master they knew so well.

Though the men were dangerous, Morgan wasn't concerned about his safety, for he trusted the King. Every evening he met with the band of brothers and together they lifted their voices to the One who cares about both the orphan and the hungry soul, no matter how much baggage they have.

As the voyage west continued, Morgan was asked to bring Words of Life to other passengers. Whether top deck with Mr. Millard and his crowd, or below with Frank, Betty, Ted, and the children, everyone seemed hungry for the King. With a revival of sorts, neither barriers of age, language, belief, or background stopped people from yearning for the King—especially the children. What Morgan possessed through holy actions had become the most valuable commodity aboard the *Iron Mistress.*

All too soon the voyage would end. Morgan pressed further into the King's call, for the future of many lives were at stake. Ready for the day, Cap'n Jack encouraged Morgan to invite all the guests to remain in the dining quarters after the meal for a special program.

After dinner, as the guests were enjoying the entertainment, the Captain called Morgan to address the group. Though Morgan was young, the Captain was certain he should speak about the King. "The people are ready to hear the truth. Be sure to invite them to receive Him, for He desires to be in relationship with every person," encouraged Cap'n Jack.

Morgan didn't spare words. "You must lay down your life, take up your cross, and follow the King." When Morgan finished speaking, Wisdom wooed them to his heart overflowing with love. The people in the room quietly reflected on the words they had heard, considering the options and what it meant to give up their old lifestyle. For Mr. Millard and his crowd, that included their livelihood.

Wholesome tranquility reigned as they listened to the waves gently lapping against the ship, the mysterious music of the ocean. A human chorus followed as everyone stood, responding in faith. "Yes!" They shouted with tears of joy streaming down their faces and called from the depth of their soul. "Come, heavenly King. Save. Heal.

Deliver. Transform all that has been futile; instead, infuse us with your glorious purpose."

It was getting late so Frank and Betty, teary-eyed, took the children to their quarters. Most of the adults remained until early the next morning doing business of a totally distinct nature that would forever change their destiny.

Once the new day dawned, Mr. Millard and his men brought all their unholy cargo from the bowels of the *Iron Mistress* and dumped every crate overboard. As each one was emptied, the men thrilled in delight mingled with doubt about the uncertain future. Not Mr. Millard. Firm in all his affairs, he knew the King was calling him to a total change of heart.

The burdensome chains of oppression to the Game Master were snapped off. The power the Game Master held on them went overboard with the last of the goods. The men shouted praise to the Chief Shepherd, delighting in their new found freedom and choosing never to return to the old way of life. Though a tremendous financial loss, it was more than worth it for life eternal is great gain indeed.

Possessing a brand new future, they gathered with the band of brothers to seek direction in this newfound way. First, old affiliations had to be dissolved, starting with the people who were waiting in great anticipation for the children. As for the contraband lying at the bottom of the sea, Mr. Millard told the brothers he could almost hear the hot angry voices tumbling out their mad desire of expectations that would not be met.

The King revealed His will to the new believers through His Holy Word. He said:

"All authority in heaven and on earth has been given to me. Therefore go and make disciples of all nations, baptizing them in the name of the Father and of the Son and of the Holy Spirit, and teaching them to obey everything I have commanded you. And surely I am with you always, to the very end of the age."[7]

"Go to all whom I send you to," said the King.

---

7   (Matthew 28:18-20).

The men were electric with anticipation. They were accepted in the Beloved and people given to the cruelty of the Game Master. Not many lovers of the King had this kind of access to the dark side of the soul. That place was their work.

Because it was the last night, Mr. Millard and his men joined the band of brothers as they assembled topside under the heavens. The task ahead was beyond human ability. They needed supernatural help to escape the cavern of depravity they trafficked in, stuck in the black hole of sordid crime. Without Wisdom, they would be overpowered, but with Him, they were unstoppable. The King gave His will and vision to the group—"life unceasing and full of glory." Mr. Millard and his men had a new employer, a new product, and a new method of operation. As they called on His help, in a moment He wiped away all their objections convincing them everything would work out well.

Morgan knew he must remain aboard the *Iron Mistress* for an uncertain period of time. He wrote a letter to the Shepherd back home to receive these men once they settled their messy affairs and help them in their calling given by the King. He then gave the note to Mr. Millard. That last night of the voyage was as heaven on earth. The cross before them and the world behind them brought assurance and comfort to all. While waiting on the King, Frank, Betty, and Morgan were given instructions to return the children to their parents back in Asia. As Morgan reflected on his seafaring life, he could never in his wildest dreams have expected to experience such happiness.

They were all going a way they never thought existed prior to meeting the King. Now He was their Way, Truth and Life, leading directly to Abba's heavenly door. With no other way being forever changed, there was no desire to turn back. They knew if they did, they would be as Lot's wife, who became a pillar of salt when attempting to return to Sodom and Gomorrah. That was not an option.

Chapter 13
Returning to Asia

Mr. Millard and his men's old way of life had exhausted itself. Though accumulating many bad behaviors, Chuck Millard found himself comforted with these words.

"Son," the King said, "Today and always, I want you to know that I see you. I see the path you've made that's all your own. I see the many unique talents and gifts you have to share. I see your brilliance, your enthusiasm, and how deeply you care and even hurt sometimes. I also see your hard-earned wisdom, destroyed innocence, courage, and compassion. What a difference you will make in this world as you follow Me. I hope you know how much I love you, and how proud I'll always be to have a son as wonderful as you." [8]

Chuck Millard's new faith was magnificently vivid compared to previously living intentionally at odds with the Master of Creation. Relinquish his power or will? Never would he have weakened himself like that! Little did he realize how much he had given away by serving the Game Master: Peace, sanity, freedom ... love? A man of his vast influence was used to having anything he desired at the snap of his fingers, anything, that is, but love. Equating love to fantasy, he let others chase that elusive ghost for that was all upside down to him. Instead, perverting love to lust was where he excelled. Just look at the nature of his business.

Surprisingly, Mr. Millard was neither sad about the loss nor concerned for the future after cutting all ties with the past by dumping the illegal cargo overboard. Instead he was filled with sorrow from the shame over the way he had lived. The only out was to follow the King and reclaim what was lost through honest labor, with ears and eyes wide open to the King's instruction. Morgan's Shepherd was the man to help Mr. Millard reclaim what the locust and canker-worm had eaten.

---

8   From AGC, Inc.

With Morgan's letter in hand, Mr. Millard gathered his men, giving the parting instructions to Frank and Betty to take back the children to Asia aboard the *Iron Mistress*. Once returned, they were to read a letter he gave them explaining why. The money they received from the original transaction was Mr. Millard's gift to the family with hopes it would help them start over. Frank and Betty were designated to check on the families periodically to be sure the children were cared for.

As Mr. Millard disembarked from the *Iron Mistress*, he turned back to Morgan and shouted, "I'll be back, not in service to myself or the Game Master any more, but only the King."

Morgan watched as the new believers disappeared into the crowd, keenly aware he must keep out of sight at this port for there was still a bounty over his head. Dismissed from unloading and reloading the ship, he went straight to his bunk, lay down in exhaustion and drifted into a deep sleep.

It was late that night when he finally awoke. Having missed both meals and the treasured time with the band of brothers, he got up and went topside so as not to disturb his cabin mates. In the moonless sky with the stars twinkling in celestial dance, Morgan lay down on deck taking in the majesty of creation, privileged to be part of His living masterpiece. Morgan's heart sang with praise as his thoughts turned to the Word of Life. He sang the Words another young man named David penned centuries ago:

The heavens declare the glory of God; the skies proclaim the work of his hands. Day after day they pour forth speech; night after night they display knowledge. There is no speech or language where their voice is not heard. Their voice goes out into all the earth, their words to the ends of the world. In the heavens he has pitched a tent for the sun, which is like a bridegroom coming forth from his pavilion, like a champion rejoicing to run his course. It rises at one end of the heavens and makes its circuit to the other; nothing is hidden from its heat.

The law of the King is perfect, reviving the soul. The statutes of the King are trustworthy, making wise the simple. The precepts of the King are right, giving joy to the heart.

The commands of the King are radiant, giving light to the eyes. The fear of the King is pure, enduring forever. The ordinances of the King are sure and altogether righteous. They are more precious than gold, than much pure gold; they are sweeter than honey, than honey from the comb. By them is your servant warned; in keeping them there is great reward.

Who can discern his errors? Forgive my hidden faults. Keep your servant also from willful sins; may they not rule over me. Then will I be blameless, innocent of great transgression.

May the words of my mouth and the meditation of my heart be pleasing in your sight, O King, my Rock and my Redeemer. [9]

Morgan was lost in worship, filled with delight, though a bit heady from the eternal victory just won. Many challenges lay ahead for the new believers, yet Morgan was confident the King was able to take them through. As the *Iron Mistress* forged into the unknown, Morgan contentedly entered his uncertain future living one day at a time following the King.

Though many saw him as an orphan with no hope, that wasn't so, for he was the exact opposite—a child of the King; anointed, blessed, and loved, possessing the greatest wealth in the world. Best of all, He would never leave nor forsake him. Morgan spent an unforgettable night in blissful fellowship with his cherished Savior.

That return voyage to Asia was a blur of activity. Morgan was given the gift to care for the children, precious lives returned from the grave to their parents. This amazing outcome completely baffled his natural thought process as he pondered how the King had brought such a total change of direction to this impossible situation.

9   Psalm 19. "LORD" changed to "King" for purposes of narrative.

Since the children's situation was totally different on this return to Asia, Frank and Betty often took them topside to play in the fresh ocean air. The children were content and free.

Arriving at their destination, Frank, Betty, and Morgan disembarked to give back the children to their parents. The whole group went to each home visiting the confused parents, of course until they heard the letter read to them from Mr. Millard. The promise of life was spoken to each household. Frank interpreted as Morgan relayed the message of Hope. That day, seven households were filled with joy as their lost child was restored to them. Couples who were embittered because they sold their child were given a new start.

Frank and Betty chose to stay in the village as their way of giving back what they had taken for so many years. Though new in faith, they heard Wisdom call them to a life of restoration. The Shepherd from Morgan's hometown would one day send helpers to this impoverished people, but as they waited, the sincere couple wanted to tell of the compelling power of this Savior. Who else could take a life that was completely corrupt as theirs had been and miraculously change it?

The whole community knew of Mr. Millard's criminal dealings, how he trafficked in illegal crops and buying and selling young souls. That these children were returned was astonishing to everyone. In the past, many parents lost their minds from the guilt of exchanging the life of their child for degradation. Since these great happenings, the same parents gave honor to the King and many returned to their senses. The townsfolk followed Frank and Betty wherever they went asking, "Tell us about this great King. We must know Him."

Morgan spoke to the people as Frank translated and lives were forever changed. Just as the children were returned to their parents, hungry souls were returned to the Chief Shepherd. Someone informed Frank a tragedy had occurred in their absence. The family of a remaining youngster was burned to death in a house fire. Everyone in the house perished, thus leaving the child an orphan. The boy, only three years old, was of no help in the fields. Who would care for him? No one wanted another mouth to feed.

An elderly woman told them she had heard of a family in the next village whose child had died recently. Though still mourning, maybe they would be suitable parents. She would take them there; besides, it was no more than an afternoon's walk. Frank, Betty, Morgan, the elderly lady, and the young boy set out to their house.

When they arrived, the young couple was working in the garden. The elderly guide explained the situation and the couple gratefully agreed to adopt the boy as their own. Only heaven could give one as precious as he was to them, and they named the child *Todd*, for it rhymed with God. The couple was quite wealthy and insisted on giving a large sum of money for him. Morgan refused until they suggested it be used for starting a center to train the community about the King.

That night they had a banquet in honor of the King for bringing this new family member to them. The servants cared for their every need at the great celebration as one course followed the next at the lavish feast.

Everyone went to sleep satisfied. Wisdom spoke the following words as they slept: "Many desire My attention, not My affection, for love requires relationship. Relationship, as you know is very expensive in time and dedication."

Next morning they told each other the mutual message from the King. Turning to Morgan, they asked, "What do we do? How do we cultivate this relationship Wisdom is speaking of? Better yet, why should we? How is this for our good?"

As Frank interpreted, Morgan said, "The King sees. Be honest. His word says, 'Nothing in all creation is hidden from God's sight. Everything is uncovered and laid bare before the eyes of him to whom we must give account.'"[10]

"Gather frequently with Him and trustworthy members of His kingdom, and read His Holy Word daily, for these are the instructions for contentment. Live it out and help each other be accountable to what it says. Most important, be with Him. Pour out your heart to the King whether you are shouting, weeping or rejoicing. He never said life would be easy, but with Him, it will be worth it. Daily live in

---

10   Hebrews 4:13.

His presence, and you'll be overwhelmed with joy at His ways. So be holy as He is holy; though temptations may assail you. Turn to Him, for He can always be trusted.

"He knows and understands and is the only One who can save us. The biggest challenge is putting aside our pride and fear for we are so easily deceived in thinking He doesn't care. This is a favorite trick of the Game Master and the farthest thing from the truth!

"Our Father yearns for us to return to Him in the relationship He alone fulfills. We often get caught attempting to satisfy ourselves through our own ways. When you want to do so, I encourage you to access the deepest yearning of your heart. Last night is a perfect example because the uncertainty of what would happen to Todd was of great concern to all of us. That desperation before we connected with you to become a new family is a sample of how Abba yearns for relationship with us, calling, "Come to Me, I Am your True Love."

"Return not to a place or the person you were, but who He made you to be. He molds and shapes us through our life experience and the day He calls us home over the vast expanse of the heavens, we shall see His face and be filled with indescribable joy. We'll have Eternity together, perfectly restored to wholeness.

"Respond to the longing in your heart, for this is a personal invitation from the Lover of your soul to be with Him. Daily I live this way, which along brings great satisfaction to each moment. This is my interpretation of the words Wisdom spoke to us last night when He said, 'Many desire My attention, not My affection, for that requires relationship. And relationship is very expensive in time and dedication.'"

When Morgan finished speaking, arrangements were made for Frank and Betty to stay with Todd's adopted parents while the center was being built. Willingly they did so in service to their King, and to help answer this young couple's many questions about Him. The location chosen for the center was where Todd's family home had been destroyed from the fire. "What better way to bring courage to a community that has been without hope for so long," Morgan said. It would become a training center of the King's Word and a place where goods could be bartered. The people would have a new livelihood, instead of raising crops of destruction.

This transformation would bring real life as an unexpected benefit to the community. Wisdom revealed from the Holy Book how to care for the land, though, of course those details would later have to happen without Morgan. After sharing these truths, he and the elderly guide said goodbye. His role aboard the *Iron Mistress* awaited him, for the sea was calling him back.

Chapter 14
Anger and Jealousy Try to Sneak In

Walking back to the ship, Morgan and his elderly guide pondered the happenings of the last few days of tragedy to triumph. Strangely, Morgan was in a slump and rather than rejoice for Todd and the community's potential from the intervention, he felt resentful. Knowing this was wrong didn't seem to matter. Every step caused Morgan's anger and jealousy to become more intense. He boarded the vessel, and by the end of the ship's workday all he wanted to do was hide under the blankets and sleep.

Others attempted to ask him what had occurred in town. He barely muttered, "Too tired to talk about it."

Finally, Cap'n Jack confronted Morgan, "What's eating you up, son?" Morgan couldn't reply as tears welled up, not quite falling from his eyes. The Captain asked, "Do you want to talk about it?"

Morgan could only shake his head because of the lump in his throat. The root of the conflicting emotions was jealousy toward Todd for receiving everything Morgan ever wanted. Why Todd and not him? Loving parents, a future filled with opportunity, the best of everything. The world belonged to Todd. As for Morgan, there weren't parents, money, home, or family. Even worse, he was a fugitive wanted by criminals trying to reclaim him as a slave to the drug trade. Why couldn't he have even a drop of the happiness Todd received? This overwhelming jealousy caused Morgan such shame he couldn't even talk with the King about it. Morgan believed he was powerless to change.

Cap'n Jack invited Morgan to wait with him on the King. After a while, the Spirit prompted Cap'n Jack to say, "Morgan, this battle within you is of the Game Master's tactics. You've been fighting an invisible war that rescued many souls from his grip. Think back on the wisdom and authority released as you spoke to those trapped in the labyrinth of the Game Master's schemes. Those words changed not just me and others, but Mr. Millard.

"Remember, long ago the Game Master was the smartest of the King's pupils. But since he rebelled, his primary aim is to steal, kill and destroy whomever he can, striving to crown himself ruler instead. As the Holy Word says:

How you have fallen from heaven, O morning star, son of the dawn! You have been cast down to the earth, you who once laid low the nations! You said in your heart, "I will ascend to heaven; I will raise my throne above the stars of God; I will sit enthroned on the mount of assembly, on the utmost heights of the sacred mountain. I will ascend above the tops of the clouds; I will make myself like the Most High." But you are brought down to the grave, to the depths of the pit.[11]

"We cannot compete with him in our own strength because he will always overpower us. Do not be discouraged dear child, the King understands and that is why He says in His Holy Word: 'Submit yourselves, then, to God. Resist the devil, and he will flee from you.'[12] My question to you, Morgan is, in what way is the King calling you to submit to Him? Where are you presently trapped by the Game Master?"

The Captain challenged Morgan to search his heart and be honest with the King. The wise Captain prayed for Morgan, and then sent him to work topside for a few days.

Morgan refinished part of the wood deck, fully immersed in the project of replacing rotting boards, sanding then varnishing the new wood. The work was therapeutic and as time wore on, Wisdom revealed Morgan was like those unprotected planks of wood without his spiritual armor. He must be equipped and prepared for battle in order to overcome the Game Master's schemes.

---

11   Isaiah 14:12-15
12   The Captain is quoting James 4:7.

Morgan was now ready to speak with the King about the rotten part of his own life. Choosing to no longer accept the Game Master's lies, Morgan believed and put on the holy armor to prepare for war according to the King's strength, not his own. Morgan glimpsed within his tormented soul pieces of his dark past-exposed roots of rage and shards of brokenness.

The King forgave Morgan the hate of his heart as the young man willingly gave the pain to Him, saying, "The only way to be free of the Game Master's deception is put on the belt of truth and be honest regarding all your struggles." The King sealed this truth to Morgan's heart by sending an eagle as a visual message. Looking up, Morgan watched the mature eagle soar the horizon and land on a dead tree close to shore. The eagle was chattering, peering toward the sea. Seemingly out of nowhere, two juvenile eagles appeared and dove into the waves, presumably after a fish in response to the direction from the perched adult. Both juveniles came up empty. One after the other perched with their backs to the water on the tree where Papa Eagle sat. Once the two juveniles were situated, the three of them began chattering, but since there was no movement from the juveniles, the chattering stopped. Morgan perceived the conversation was a family fishing lesson. Papa, the provider, was teaching the juveniles how to fish, and it was time the youngsters learn how to do so themselves.

They followed Papa Eagle's instruction, but had missed the mark—it was an honest mistake that happens to everyone occasionally. The problem arose once the juveniles perched on that dead tree. Their choice was made; they weren't going to be humiliated again. "Dad is capable of catching dinner for us, so we'll just wait for him to do it," they seemed to say by their inaction. But that was not going to happen.

Papa Eagle advised, "Go again. Watch, wait. Keep trying. You'll get your fish." But those youngsters were set with backs to the water, choosing to ignore his advice. That is when all conversation ceased between Papa and his children.

I see how similar Papa Eagle is to my heavenly Papa, Morgan realized. Then Morgan heard his heavenly Papa speak:

You're young and missed the mark by letting anger and jealousy set in. Now you are recovering your dignity here on a perch I created in order to speak with you, son. Humble yourself, then dust yourself off, you're forgiven. These experiences, as well as others down the way, are for your growth. Talk to My people about these things. Humiliation comes from brokenness mingled with taunts from the Game Master. That is when My people attempt to isolate and disregard My call. What about you? What are you going to do, Morgan?

My will for you is to rescue the perishing as a fisher of men. Have I not called you to this? Arise! Come out of the death's dark cave and live. Everyone is waiting. Me, you, My people. Don't fear. I am with you. It is not your ability anyhow, but Mine. Don't get stuck like those young eagles, which are like so many of My children. Instead, turn back to the sea, set your sight on the harvest, then at My command, dive! But to rescue, not devour. Learning shall occur as long as you are on this earth. Enjoy the process. Wait, listen, and then do as I say. Even the complex is easy when you go with Me.

Morgan could almost feel the Father's embrace as He continued. "I love you. Peace is found in Me alone." Though just a short time had passed, it seemed an eternity, for the heaviness he had been suffering over his short lifetime was gone. Morgan's heart was clean yet again.

That night with the band of brothers, he confessed what had occurred. Though this was Old Steward's first visit, he must speak, for he couldn't hide his feelings any longer. Shame tried to overcome him but Morgan remembered Papa's fishing lesson. It was his turn to dive and tell how the King had brought healing out of pain.

Afterward, one of the guys asked the group, "Does anyone else have a need before we pray for Morgan?" The Old Steward cleared his throat. Starting softly, quickly gaining volume and momentum, he poured out his story about his years of debauchery. "The scent of the ocean lured this old sailor by her exotic mystery. But beneath that veneer of whim and wonder, a hard reality loomed."[13]

---

13   This quotation is from a true story. See the *Seattle Times* A1. February 23, 2011.

Continuing with broken speech he said, "The crime; neglect of wife ... my kids needed me ... doing my own thing instead ... wicked things ... the angel? ... almost dead ... jobless... Cap'n Jack ... Last twenty years I tried to get my wife and kids back—start over. I guess I just botched it up too much. Some things can't be fixed—my life, doing the same things, hoping to get what I want. Not so. I must take responsibility at some point. I don't want to cover up anymore. When I did it my way it was empty, even in a room full of loot. Yeah, I pirated the high seas as a young man. Empty, hollow life and in the process, I am all used up. You guys are different though. You have challenges, but you change. I need that. I can't keep living this dead end anymore.

"Memories haunt me constantly. In the daytime I relive the harm I've done. Nothing makes the pain go away—you can believe I've tried everything. Drinking, women, even rubbing the bellies of mute statues. The worst part is nighttime, though. Demons attack as I toss and turn; terrified, I try not to sleep, but exhaustion eventually overtakes me. That is when the nightmares come. They start with the good time memories. The fun I had back then, the wild, raucous nights of wine, women, and song. Wading through piles of gold coins and throwing the plunder we had stolen up in the air with glee. Next, I'm in a courtroom. The judge is questioning my victims one after another as a deck of cards fanned out before me. I watch as each person I harmed walks past, stopping to look right into my eyes before moving on. It is an eerie feeling. Some of them cry, and then memories flood my mind of what I did to them. I beg the judge and jury to overlook my crimes—some very heinous crimes.

"The gavel falls as the Judge declares, 'Not guilty.' Then He turns to me and adds, 'How long shall you continue doing the same thing? Defying Me, harming My people, and getting away with it? How long before you change your ways?'

"Then I wake up in a cold sweat, shaking all over. This nightly dream used to bring me joy that I was cleared of guilt, now it fills me with terror. I never used to care until I met that little girl, or angel—whatever she was. I told Morgan how that encounter changed my life. Now I see though never tried in human court, before heaven's tribunal I am condemned.

"No one knows this, but my eldest son followed my footsteps to become a drunk that wasn't satisfied with just whiskey. Nope, over-lapped into psychedelic drugs and in short order got him a wet brain. You know what that is, don't you? Dead spots up there; one minute he's doing something and then boom, out he falls. He says and does weird things all the time. His emotions and actions are out of control. He's alive, but never will he know the love of a good woman, or have kids, for that matter.

"Refusing medical attention, he lives like a wild man in the for-est eating whatever he can find, I reckon. No one can get close to him, especially me. Not because I haven't tried. It's just that I am helpless to stop him from throwing rocks, and clawing at himself. That's just one of my eight kids. They all have lots of troubles, far as I can tell. Yup, I'm not behind bars as I deserve, but I'm paying. So guys, tell me, would this King bother with a salty old dog like me?"

They responded, "There is no other name by which men can be saved. We have all sinned and fallen short of His glory. Do you believe?"

"Yes," he replied.

The other men remained silent as one of the deck hands spoke. "Being a parent can be overwhelming. Just think of each of your children as you raised them, loving them your way, later striving to reclaim their love. It is exasperating even in the best of situations. As our loving parent, Abba Father has a special place in His heart for the backslider. You know what it means to treat Him defiantly. The dream you've described is Wisdom, desiring to grant love and for-giveness to you. Your part is to acknowledge your mistakes, ask His pardon and repent. That means turn away from your old ways and attitudes, ask His forgiveness, and turn to Him. He wants to reside in your heart, don't you hear Him calling?"

"Yes, yes," said Old Steward. "I hear."

"'Come now, let us reason together,' says the Lord. 'Though your sins are like scarlet, they shall be as white as snow; though they are red as crimson, they shall be like wool. If you are willing and obedient, you will eat the best from the land; but if you resist and rebel, you will be devoured by the sword.' For the mouth of the Lord has spoken."[14]

When he was through speaking, all the men began a chorus of praise, interceding for Old Steward while looking into their own souls.

After a while Morgan relayed this message from the King. "Such pain we create in our quest to satisfy our desires. Born perfect, each cell functions perfectly, but without relationship with our Beloved, self-will drives us and we end up destroying our beautiful bodies and minds. He calls us back for He loves us more than we'll ever know. At some point in our lives we hear Him say, "When the pain and sorrow overwhelms I will be there for you to lean on. Call to Me, grasp Wisdom as I pull you out of the miry pit you've chosen.'"

Eventually, the men retired to their cabins, but not Old Steward. He remained in the presence of the Heavenly Judge basking in forgiveness, being made whole. Finally free he told his beloved King, "You're the best thing that ever happened to me!"

Morgan was forgotten by the band of brothers. But it was enough they had listened to his confession to bring forth the necessary transformation. Morgan lay in his bunk and listened intently before drifting off to sleep. The King spoke quietly to his spirit:

My beloved son, you are the apple of My eye, My pearl of great price. I made you just for Me, to live with Me and be with Me every moment. I know you are absorbing this way of living with all your might. There has been much I have had to educate you about. My Kingdom ways are tremendously different from those of this world. You are not being disciplined for something you've done wrong.

No way! You are being blessed with My way of life eternal now on this earth. I see in you a man who desires Me with all his heart, mind, strength, and soul. As a result, I give Myself to you! Do not fear this world, its people or its ways. I am your King walking with you every day. I am taking care of you. Every experience, every moment is for your very best. I have designed it this way because I love you.

14   Isaiah 1:18-20.

Do you hear me? I said I love you! It's OK, Morgan. I want you to let out all the poison. You know the hurt, loss and incomprehensible pain from the ways of this world. It is not what I desire for you, I never did. Your human frailty picked it up as a result of life experiences. Confusion is not from Me. Son, I want you to be My ambassador to the nations, soul by soul. Don't be concerned how, or what that is to look like, just be obedient.

Soak Me in. Enjoy being My beloved one, belonging to Me. I have much for you in the days ahead. Your path and what it looks like belongs to Me. Just work for Me. Keep being honest. I love that you're as pure and trusting as a child. My heart is embracing you. Everywhere you turn, there I am. The best part is this is what we both want.

I long for you and you long for Me. Do you realize how holy this is? All too often, love is only one-sided—I for My people. They only want Me in part. To bless, heal, or change the situation from bad to good according to their need. Once all is well, they depart. They don't need Me anymore, but not you. Whether all is well, or as you prosper, you still involve Me. You look for ways to include Me in all your relationships for all reasons. You don't give up after many rejections from either those you love, or your enemies.

The best part is that you wait and listen to Me, asking for clarification, then proceeding to the best of your understanding to accomplish My will. You are honest about your weaknesses and don't cover up when you fall. I love you for all of these reasons and many more. But most of all, I love you for being you.

Morgan, this is your heavenly Abba Father, speaking to your spirit through My Spirit. Don't worry about things as they are on this earth. Nothing shall touch you. I will not allow one hair of your head to be harmed. Continue to trust Me and live for Me. You belong to Me, precious child.

Tell My people I long for this type of a love relationship with all of them. Your days on this earth, each one, shall be blessed. Extract joy from them. I am pouring out My joy from heaven to fill your heart where there used to be darkness and pain. I am filling you full of acceptance with joy. No longer shall the darkness be able to grip you.

I have only light. I am Light, I am Love and I am filling you now. Receive.

Don't worry about the changes you sense within. Though they seem negative, they are not. Rather, I am equipping you to become My ambassador, able and ready to meet any need or crisis I choose to send you into. Be sure to wait and listen to Me. Bask in Me. Enjoy the warmth and joy I bring as the summer sun. Soak Me in that way. Our private times together shall equip you for every task I call you to. I shall one day bring the perfect mate that you complement one another as you exude My heavenly love to each other and everyone around you. There is much more I desire to speak with you about. Are your ears open?

Morgan replied, "Yes, I open them and my heart wide to your voice alone, in your Name that is above every name."

The King continued:

Son, listen to Me closely. Let all other thoughts go far from you, yesterday, tomorrow, even the next moment. Instead open yourself to Me completely now. Ready? Good. Stop and be still. Soak Me in. I have created you for Me. Others have a part in your life as you do theirs, but you are Mine. Be free knowing that. Keep coming closer to Me each day. When you are weak, I shall be your strength. When you fall, I shall pick you up. When you are happy, I rejoice with you. I love you! Obey My word and do as I say. All shall be very well. *I love you!*

Morgan peacefully fell asleep. Someday he would grasp the full power of these words from Abba—he just didn't realize how soon.

Chapter 15
Time's Movin' On

Morgan continued as assistant to Old Steward aboard the *Iron Mistress*. Mr. Millard and his men had returned to Asia, only now as the King's representatives, joined by other servants of the Shepherd's flock.

Mr. Millard and his men found serving the King and His people their greatest delight. They had gratefully resigned from the old way of life, for it was all used up, and no longer attractive. They had become pilgrims on earth and strangers to the allurement of the Game Master. Tirelessly, they heeded the King's call in the Holy Book to "go and make disciples of all nations, baptizing them in the name of the Father and of the Son and of the Holy Spirit, and teaching them to obey everything I have commanded you. And surely I am with you always, to the very end of the age."[15]

The place where Todd's birth family had been killed by the fire had since become a life-giving center for the community, a birthplace to bring the lost into the kingdom of Light. Here was the workplace of Mr. Millard and his men. At the ordained time, according to the King's Spirit, they were sent out in groups of two, speaking wherever they were led.

Mr. Millard and Morgan's Shepherd worked together across the sea to bring people out of poverty into wholeness. The King told them, "I tell you, open your eyes and look at the fields! They are ripe for harvest."[16]

Though the Shepherd was on a different continent, Wisdom kept them close. Each time the *Iron Mistress* crossed the ocean, the Shepherd sent desperately needed supplies and workers back to Asia to assist there. Cap'n Jack always made sure there was room for the King's business aboard his vessel, often at his own expense.

---

15 Matthew 28:19.
16 John 4:35.

Morgan served the passengers and crew aboard the *Iron Mistress* as if they were royalty; the King had made clear that each soul is of great value to Him. Morgan was instructed by Wisdom to focus on restoring fellowship with the King and His people by serving them well. The passengers received the gift of a lifetime under his care, which included speaking Words of Life as apples of gold within settings of silver like the Holy Book said. Those who hadn't known the King before were transported not just across the ocean to different continents, but to the Kingdom of heaven, as well.

Still, Morgan ached for something more. In his mind, he saw masses beckoning him from distant lands to bring them words from the King. But first, he must learn contentment now as taught only by Wisdom. Being content would prepare him to overcome many deceitful tricks of the Game Master. Thus Morgan cultivated dedication through a listening ear and ready heart tuned exclusively to the King's voice.

"As long as you want what you can't have, you will continually be at the Game Master's mercy," the King said. Armed with truth, he hardened himself against such treachery. Besides, the King's promises were always the best. Through the process, Morgan experienced the bittersweet gift of waiting then surrendering to the King's perfect will.

Life aboard the *Iron Mistress* settled into the routine of adjusting to constant change. Winter below the equator and summer above determined how the home office scheduled her cruises. Outside of occasional dry dock for making repairs and scraping barnacles, the ship was constantly occupied. Morgan was given many opportunities to serve the King as Old Steward's assistant, while practically every evening meeting with the band of brothers.

Morgan cherished the challenges of daily walking the narrow path of the King's choosing. He no longer looked to his own understanding, recognizing his many limitations; rather, he developed a listening ear tuned to the Creator.

One morning while circling the Horn of Africa, Cap'n Jack told Morgan and Old Steward, "Get your things together. Our next port of call is where your service aboard the *Iron Mistress* shall cease. You both have a job to do in this Land of Enchantment, Africa!

"One continent possessing many nations is where you shall preach the King's message. Over the years you've responded to the Spirit's call to prepare; now you are ready. Mr. Millard and his group in Asia, along with the Shepherd's effort in North America have provided hope for many. Now you are released to help build in this soil. The King has spoken; you are ready as are the land and its people. It is time. Go!"

Overjoyed at the prospect, Morgan knelt before the King in humble gratitude as Cap'n Jack anointed him. Morgan and Old Steward packed their things. Early the next morning they would arrive at their destination. Their last night the band of brothers gathered around Morgan and Old Steward, pouring Words of Life into the deep wells of their soul. This encouraged them for the challenges they would meet ahead. They were told, "Dwell in the shelter of the Most High (and) rest in the shadow of the Almighty." [17]Whether cheery or dreary, though there may seem to be no way out as the power of hell is unleashed and crashing against you like the mighty sea, do not fear. Instead, fear Him who created all things, for He is our true hiding place that fills you with songs of deliverance. Preach the word in His strength, not yours. Be sure to take your sword and shield, constantly prepared in the Word joined with faith. Do this and all shall go well."

---

17   Psalm 91:1.

Part III
Ariel

Interlude

"Multitudes, multitudes in the valley of decision..."
Joel 3:14

Where does her story begin, now, or then? Who is she? Her name is Ariel, a woman warrior. Since there are so many angles, let's start in the beginning. Not just her beginning, but ours, collectively.

We were supposed to overcome the simple test by choosing according to the voice of the King. But we didn't, so we were kicked out of our happy home, all because of a little food choice. If only the beginners had listened to Wisdom instead of the Game Master, how different our journey would be. Everything was lush and crystal clear then, not like this harsh land that must be cultivated or it overtakes us.

This is where Ariel's journey begins. She was born forty-eight years ago in a small fishing village, an interesting yet mysterious place. Though dearly loved by her parents, they had no idea that hearing cloudy messages endangered them and would alter their previously happy lives together as a family. The disintegration could have been avoided if only they had followed the clear teaching from Wisdom's little book.

Unfortunately, His voice was lost to many in their days. Actually, Wisdom's voice gets clouded in every age. With the beginners though, the Game Master seems to present a much more exotic alternative. Who wants to plod along, following strange instructions from a dusty book, when we can fly or be like a princess or ninja? We can play any part and experience the ultimate rush of whatever fulfills the longing within. At least, that is what he deceives us into thinking.

That is what the Game Master told Ariel's parents. Their fantasies would be satisfied, or so they believed. Thus, Ariel's father prospered as an appointee of the Game Master, though they were alone in a precarious village, afloat on a boat designed by the best craftsmen there. Every village had a travel craftsman who constructed each one's unique mode of transportation, essential for the proper function of the family, for we all have to get around.

Chapter 16
Disaster Tears a Family Apart

When Ariel was four, she was playing with her three-year-old brother Sammy near the forest behind their home. Following a game of chase, they were rolling around on the grass, tickling each other and laughing hysterically. For some reason, Sammy got up suddenly and ran into the thick trees close by before Ariel realized what had happened.

Both children were familiar with their parents' clear instructions to avoid the forest because wild animals lived there. Yet Sammy disappeared into the thick underbrush and trees. Ariel screamed his name repeatedly—nothing.

Running back to the house to get her parents, she breathlessly yelled, "Sammy ... gone—forest." That was all it took and though comfortably seated on the couch one moment, they ran wildly out the door in the direction she pointed. The three of them, Mom, Dad, and Ariel, ran into the forest calling out Sammy's name, hoping to see or hear him.

Instead there was nothing but silence. Ariel thought she saw a flash of fur withdraw into the underbrush, but was unsure. Beckoning to her parents, she told them what she had seen. Starting down that path, they found a shoe, then a ripped sock. Dad gestured to Mom, "Go back to the house with Ariel, now."

Ariel felt his words cut through her like a knife. She was to blame for anything that happened to Sammy. She would never forgive herself for such a horrible crime of negligence, never.

Terrified, Mom and Ariel held each other while waiting to hear what had happened, yet not wanting to hear. It seemed forever had passed as fear and pain consumed them; then Dad arrived. Head down crying, he carrying part of Sammy's ripped shirt covered with blood. Sammy was gone. Everyone knew about those creatures that lurked in the dark places like demons running in packs that rarely left evidence.

At least they found a few items. The three of them huddled together on the floor holding the remains of Sammy's blood soaked clothes. Speechless, they cried rivers of tears through the night into the next day consumed in a pain no words could heal. Sometimes Ariel slept, but not her parents.

After a week, they buried the remains Dad found in the forest. Just the three of them, alone and overcome with grief. Neither parents said it, but Ariel's mind convinced her she was responsible. Sammy was practically a baby. She wished she had died instead. It would certainly be better than this.

Until now, the small family lived on a beautiful farm that was very productive. Both Dad and Mom were hard workers with common sense, a necessary trait for farmers. Her dad diligently worked the land from plowing to harvest producing a plentiful bounty. He then took the crops to the city by boat. Because they were so healthy, they quickly sold. With the profit, Dad filled the storehouse for the upcoming winter, purchasing necessities along with gifts of cloth for mom and toys for the kids. Sometimes there were two harvests if the season permitted.

Those were good days with plenty of laughter and happy memories. The four of them had enjoyed life wrapped up in one another. But those days were gone forever. Little whispers from the Game Master, mixed with intense grief at their loss, caused Mom and Dad to drift between tears and bitter arguments, with Dad storming off frequently. They kept working the land, but were only shells of what they had been. Recovery seemed unattainable and within the year, Mom finally ended it, asking Dad to leave.

No longer in a united family, Ariel practically disappeared. No brother, estranged parents, she hated herself for this tragedy. Though functioning on the outside, she was unable to escape the tainted memories.

Old enough, Ariel was sent to the village schoolhouse that next fall. The younger children went by ferryboat back and forth while the older ones rode horses. Everyone at school already knew about the tragedy that brought this horrible curse on her family. Between the death of her beloved brother and the disgrace of her parents' divorce, Ariel was shunned by everyone, including her teachers. Labeled an outcast, she became a quiet observer who wasn't invited to participate in childhood fun with her classmates.

Good days were when she was left alone which were few and far between. Many kids taunted her. The boys pulled her hair and the girls whispered behind her back giving "the look." On one occasion, a couple boys tried to touch her that bad way, but a teacher saw it on the playground and intervened.

She let her dad know she was being teased, so he taught her to fight and defend herself. She always thought she would look out for little Sammy, not herself. The overwhelming pain was causing her to lash out in fits of violence, especially toward boys.

When Ariel turned nine, a new girl moved to town. That is when everything changed. Vicky was well liked because of her kindness toward everyone, especially Ariel; like a burst of warm sunshine over her frozen heart a small seed of hope started to emerge.

Since her earliest memory Ariel spoke with Wisdom about the hurt in her heart. How she had looked forward to Sammy's birth, so happy to have a baby brother and friend to love. How could this disaster happen? The remembering always brought a sour feeling inside. Around she went with Wisdom who tried to comfort her, but to no avail. There came a day Vicky introduced Ariel to the King, lifting her out of the dungeon of despair to soar the heavens as those majestic eagles she admired.

Overjoyed, Ariel attempted to share her new Friend with Mom and Dad as soon as she saw them, but they weren't interested. Her Dad had a vacant look in his eye as she tried to share the love of her life, but her Mom made it clear she never wanted to hear the King's name again. So Ariel kept her treasured Friend in her heart, plus at school with Vicky. There were other girls Vicky included in their friendship that had previously been cruel to Ariel. Though they still disliked her, because she was with Vicky they tolerated her. At least she wasn't alone anymore. Not saying much, she listened and watched, painfully aware of their rejection; it seemed nothing was easy.

Sometimes she stayed with Vicky and her family on the weekends, going to church together on Sunday to kids' class learning how to live with the King in this complicated world. One autumn day, their Sunday school teacher arranged a special event for the girls. She called it "A day with the King." The teen girls were to teach the younger ones what it means to be His princess. Dressed up in lacy frills, their head teacher, Mrs. Jacqueline, led them into worship. Their teenage instructor, Lelani, encouraged them in what it means to think like a princess, not just outwardly, but from within the heart and mind. "The King's princess is one who loves others and is considerate to those less fortunate," Lelani told them. Everyone recognized that Vicky was a good example of a girl who lived that way.

"Regarding hardships," Lelani said, "They are a normal part of life. It's the direction we choose that determines our impact on earth. We are meant to leave evidence of what a holy life with the King signifies wherever we go. Breathing life into us, He washes away all death, so we can bring life to others through our words and actions. Called as royal ambassadors, we represent His Kingdom and become holy as He transforms us."

Lelani taught how to express love, saying, "If someone is mean, be kind to them. Forgive as one that cares about the King's business, His people, and His ways."

The teen girls gave white lace gloves to the young ladies before going to mid-afternoon tea in town. Upon entering the shop, they noticed a young girl sitting with adults, looking lonely as the grown-ups visited among themselves. Mrs. Jacqueline encouraged the girls to invite her to join them, saying, "That is what a princess does. When someone is left out, she invites them in."

The girls introduced themselves and asked her to join them, but she declined. When they returned, Mrs. Jacqueline asked them what the girl's name was. Having not asked, they skipped back to her table and learned her name was Susie. Practicing kindness was becoming great fun.

Settling into the pleasure of high tea with one another, the girls intentionally invited the King and Wisdom as guests of honor—or were the girls His honored guests? Either way, He delighted in their cheerful chatter as Mrs. Jacqueline led them in expressing His holy love in Spirit and truth. These girls, rescued from the kingdom of darkness into His marvelous light so young, brought His soul joy.

Before leaving the shop, Mrs. Jacqueline awarded each girl with a princess crown. She charged them to love one another as the King loves, giving of Himself and always forgiving. Going to each patron in the shop, they shared the reason for their joy—freedom in Christ! This freedom to grow and develop as intended rather than led by that cunning Game Master encouraged both them and the hearers.

The young ladies were learning to trust the King in how to treat others His way. The other girls also asked for Ariel's forgiveness at having treated her badly in the past. Lifelong friendships were forged that day as a result. Yes, challenges would come, but instead of being vulnerable, together they were prepared to overcome the Deceiver, who seeks every chance to bring disaster.

Chapter 17
A Changed Dad

Things were improving at school for Ariel. She no longer needed to fight with anyone, but at home little had changed. Her mom was always exhausted attempting to keep their small farm operating. They had recently attained a few milk goats and were making cheese and butter to sell along with the produce. This helped some although their farm hand had left after last harvest with all the profit. Though it was hard, Ariel chose to forgive him, but her Mom could not. These difficulties kept wearing her down.

Ariel was now old enough to go by horseback to school, but her Mom surely couldn't afford one. This didn't concern Ariel, who was more interested observing the wild horses run through the valley. She loved to watch them drinking water from the river's edge as the ferryboat daily took the youngsters back and forth to school.

Being a curious person, she found their favorite grazing places in the valley close by the farm. There was only fifteen in the herd, but each year their numbers grew as new foals were born. They left before the harsh winter arrived, returning at the new bud of spring when the baby grass appears.

The wild horses were comfortable around Ariel, who arrived early almost every day to watch them before doing her chores. Singing love songs to the King, she shared many sweet hours of fellowship there with Him and Wisdom. The horses felt comfortable and approached her so she could feed treats of carrots and apples from the farm's cold storage.

This day was different though. A pregnant mare was laying down giving birth in the underbrush when Ariel arrived. Ariel had never seen such a thing and watched transfixed as the little foal started coming from the mare. After a long struggle, the mare appeared exhausted, for the foal seemed to be stuck inside. Ariel recognized she needed help and ran home to get Fred, the new ranch hand. Arriving out of breath, she told him the mare was in trouble and needed help.

Together they quickly gathered up plenty of rags and a couple buckets of water. By the time they returned, the other horses had gathered around the mare.

"Yup, a breach," said Fred. "We got to move fast to save 'em." Like a surgeon, he reached inside the mare to move the foal's legs aright. Once accomplished, out the foal came covered with birth fluid yet appearing strong and healthy. Fred and Ariel washed him down since the mare was too weak to do so.

Ariel insisted she stay until the mare was better. She set up camp and brought her dog Lady while Fred went to town to get Ariel's Dad to join the vigil. Day and night they nursed the mare back to health. Putting goat milk in a bucket to feed the foal, they watched as he sucked the milk from Ariel's fingers as a substitute for the mare's teats until she was strong enough to nurse him. They also brought water and grain for the mare, and within a few days she was back on her feet grazing and caring for her young one.

Ariel and her Dad had a lot of time to talk and one evening, she shared again about her beloved King. She showed her Dad the King's love letter, the Holy Book sent from His heavenly kingdom through His chosen writers. She told him what the King had done and how He had changed everything for her.

Ariel's Dad witnessed his daughter's change, though he hadn't realized the King's part in it. His own youth had been filled with many imagined slights that caused him to blame the King. He hadn't given room in his soul to hear these truths until now. Sure, there's relative truth, yours, mine, ours, he convinced himself. *But one truth, no way.*

But a miracle happened; just as the mare received life, so Ariel's Dad received new birth in that rugged valley. Father and daughter were now united in the King—for Dad believed.

That next day, Dad put a halter around the mare, leading her and the foal back to the farm. The sun was up mid-sky as they approached the small farm, and Mom was in the garden pulling weeds. She looked up to see Ariel and her Dad leading the recovering mare, with the foal following. Fred pulled the small cart that held their belongings from the week's vigil.

As they got closer, Ariel noticed her Mom's pain encrusted eyes appeared teary with a slight quiver on her lower lip. Mom didn't take her eye off Dad while asking questions about the horses. It had been a long time since they had a civil conversation, actually not since the divorce. Ariel thought she noticed her Dad's eyes seemed damp as they talked.

"Restored and whole," Dad cleared his throat then commented, referring to the mare and his soul. Ariel led the horses to the barn where the other animals were kept to give her parents a chance to talk. While Ariel and her Dad were in the valley caring for the horses, Fred had built a corral by the barn. One horse was hard to come by for most folks, but they had two, a gold mine for this struggling family. "These horses will be the catalyst that forever changes our lives," Dad predicted.

Dad remained long past dinner that night talking with Mom, as they opened their hearts to each other, releasing the pain from their imprisoned souls. For the first time in years, Ariel had hope for her wounded family. Surprisingly, next morning Dad was at breakfast. He had stayed overnight in the workers' cabins and remained to set right the affairs on the farm. As a result, Mom breathed easier with him resuming many of the responsibilities. After a while, Dad went to town with a windfall crop, just what they needed to get out of debt. He brought not only winter supplies, but also a few belongings upon returning.

That night after dinner, Dad gave Ariel a beautiful bridle for the mare along with a grooming kit. Then he turned to Mom and gave her a small package with a fancy bow and card attached. She opened it with anticipation to reveal a Holy Book with her name embossed on the cover. Dad had written inside, "To the woman I will love forever. Will you remarry me"? Before she could respond, he got on his knees and proposed a second time.

She exclaimed, "Yes!" Shouts of joy filled the room as the family celebrated their life being fully restored.

The preparations for the wedding brought a flurry of activity between sewing dresses, sending invitations, and the Shepherd's premarital instructions. The date was set for mid-September, the same as when they were first married. This time, everything was different, for they were walking with the King and a whole community of believers. No longer alone, horrible memories from the past were washed away, replaced with the assurance they were accepted in the Beloved.

Ariel was more secure than ever. Becoming both a lady and a scholar, she paid closer attention to her teachers and they paid close attention to her. It was obvious to everyone the King was molding her early challenges into a life of great value. Ariel had one desire, to bring Him glory. She started her day with Wisdom, singing love songs like, "Search me, O God, and know my heart; test me and know my anxious thoughts. See if there is any offensive way in me, and lead me in the way everlasting."[18] She was radiant after spending time with Him.

The mare had fully recovered and was responding well to her training in the corral. The colt trotted beside his mother during these lessons, their coats glistening in the sun. After school, Ariel brushed them daily, giving them just a little grain along with a carrot or apple to supplement their grazing. She checked on the herd often; in a few short weeks they would depart for winter.

Fred and Ariel trained the mare in the corral. Though not ready for the open field, Ariel hoped to run her with the other horses when the herd returned in the spring. They must remain free. She couldn't bear for those stately animals to become beasts of labor.

It was a busy time, with only a couple weeks until the wedding. Ariel and Mom were working hard to finish sewing the elegant bridal

18   Ariel's prayer comes from Psalm 139:23-24.

gowns. Soft pink with classic lines for Ariel; white with lace trim on the bodice and a full-length veil for Mom, not to mention the dresses for the bridesmaids. Dad stayed in the workers' quarters until the wedding. Since all past contracts with the Game Master were demolished, they chose to wait until after the ceremony to be together as man and wife.

Finally, the day arrived. Mom and Ariel were dressed in their gowns as Mrs. Jacqueline, Vicky, and the bridesmaids helped with the finishing touches. The church was decorated with flowers. White lace sashes adorned seven lit candelabras lining the aisle Mom would soon walk down to reunite in holy matrimony with Dad. It had been years since they dwelled under the same roof. Soon the estrangement would end.

Dad was standing in a tux next to Fred, his best man and trusted friend. Dad was ready to be reunited to his true love. As Mom started walking down the aisle, everyone turned to behold the beautiful bride. Dad straightened up immediately and from that moment on, Mom and Dad's eyes never parted. Mom's dad was no longer alive, so Vicki's dad walked Mom down the aisle to present her to the waiting groom. A holy hush filled the church and from beginning to end, each soul present was profoundly affected, for the whole town had been watching this little family.

Prayers of faith that won this battle were fought at a great cost to many, especially Ariel. Though the results were a delight to her heart, painful wounds still remained. Present among the candlesticks was the Chief Physician, filled with tremendous satisfaction, beaming blessings upon them.

It had been twenty years since Mom and Dad had exchanged their first wedding vows. When the Shepherd said, "You may now kiss the bride," Dad unreservedly embraced the small of her back and kissed her. The whole assembly cheered so loudly it seemed the roof would come off. Joyous rejoicing followed in a festival of praise. Then everyone went downstairs to enjoy a special feast prepared for the occasion.

The church bell later rang when the carriage pulled up to whisk Mom and Dad away to a small country bungalow for their honeymoon. As Mom and Dad held hands walking down the stairs of the church, the guests bordered them and threw rice on the happy couple. Mom turned as the crowd spilled out of the church behind them, quickly filling the stairway onto the front lawn. Before tossing the bridal bouquet, Mom caught her daughter's attention. Ariel noticed that years of sorrow had been erased from Mom's face and it seemed from her heart, as well. Her eyes and face reflected the peace of letting go.

She blew a kiss to her daughter and whispered, "I love you," through the crowd. Though silent, Ariel heard its echo as though her Mom had yelled it through a loudspeaker. Mom then threw the bridal bouquet, which was caught by a young girl laughing in anticipation. That act described Ariel's experience of receiving forgiveness from her parents. Years of oppression and self-hate regarding Sammy's death instantly melted away.

As they stepped into the carriage, the driver gave the reins to Dad, who clicked his tongue and off they went. That moment marked the beginning of their new life together. The King had spoken to Ariel before about forgiving herself, but she hadn't been able to. Ariel understood that in even the best situation, horrible things happen beyond anyone's control, but the memories continued to haunt her. Still, He had been doing a hidden work of healing the pain from Ariel's heart for some time.

Reflecting about these matters, Ariel looked up and realized she was now alone. With her parents long gone, she made a decision that changed her life forever; to accept the King's offer of forgiveness as fact. She wanted to spend her days loving others into His eternal Kingdom and if He could forgive her, He could do anything for anyone. While they communed together, He made it clear that the only way to reach the dark chasm of a human soul is to obey Him. His voice told her spirit, "By this all men will know you are my disciples, if you love one another."[19]

Ariel wouldn't forget the King's healing, having received love wrapped in forgiveness. She realized we choose to value others as He does to show this generation who He truly is. It is mind-boggling

19   The words of Jesus in John 13:35.

how people search for Him in the wrong places following the wrong paths.

Wisdom then leaned over and kissed her forehead, anointing her with His heavenly call. She was filled with a love like never before to tell people about the One who can do anything—even take away shame, and replace it with new life. She promised, "I choose one day at a time to live for You, my Beloved One."

In that moment, Ariel's attitude changed from thinking only of herself to becoming the King's servant. She surrendered her life to the only One who could fulfill His purpose in her. There would be ongoing struggles, so she must seek His direction to overcome victoriously.

The first week of her parent's honeymoon, Ariel stayed with Vicky's family and went to school. That Sunday after church, she returned home to help on the farm. Fred now worked diligently on the grounds since harvest had passed. There was a leak in the chicken shed that needed patching up, and some of the fences needed to be rebuilt too. Ariel milked the goats, fed the chickens, and collected the eggs. After finishing her homework she trained with the mare and colt.

Riding the mare in the small corral was getting boring, but Ariel was learning patience in the process. What she really longed for was to run the horses in the open field.

Falling off the horse had been part of those sessions, but Ariel wasn't ready for the mare to do what she did. Walking went just fine until Ariel instructed the horse to trot. That's when the mare ran full speed then stopped abruptly and started bucking wildly until Ariel was on her neck halfway to the ears. Ariel set herself straight and rode the mare the remaining length of the pasture. Though a rocky start, Ariel and the mare now understood one another and from that point on, the mare accepted her rider.

Ms. Jacqueline stayed at the farm while her parents were gone to look after Ariel until they returned. Once dinner was ready, she called Fred and Ariel in to wash up and sit down to a nourishing meal of hot chili and fresh vegetables from the garden. There was a beautiful fresh baked loaf of brown bread with hand churned goat butter.

The three of them bowed their heads, thanking their Maker for His bounty and blessings, as the delicious smells from the hot meal filled the room.

In October, the days were getting shorter with the sun filling the room with its golden hue. Candles were lit, for it would be dark before dinner was over. The room was filled with peace as the three of them enjoyed the meal, recounting the recent events. Ariel shared the day's training of the mare. Relieved she wasn't hurt, they laughed heartily, visualizing the scene.

Fred would be finished with the chicken coop soon. Tonight was his turn to milk the goats, thus ending another honest day's work at the farm. As for working with the horses, they agreed spring was a better time to run the mare with the herd. Fred had an idea to breed her to help the little farm financially. After the colt was trained next year, he would bring a good price at the market. This year Ariel could train the mare and colt together.

Ariel loved animals and was grateful they didn't raise any for the butcher. Just a few chickens and an occasional wild deer provided enough meat for their needs, supplemented by fish caught at the river nearby. Though their primary trade was eggs and goat milk products along with fresh produce, Fred had recently planted a few acres of fruit trees. After waiting three years for the trees to mature according to the King's instructions, the family was confident they would be ready for an abundant harvest.

Since Fred arrived, there had been plenty of changes for the little family. A fellow believer, he and Ariel spoke often about the King, though Mom and Dad resisted in the past. Like an uncle, Fred explained how to overcome the challenges of attempting to live holy in a world filled with sin. Rather than becoming discouraged, Ariel was strengthened to keep the faith. Everything had changed since Ariel's parents were reunited and one.

Fred went out to finish up the evening chores and as he walked to the barn, the setting sun left behind the first sprinkling of stars to light the night sky. On this night of the new moon, the sky would soon be filled with the stars' beauty twinkling above.

Inside, Ms. Jacqueline and Ariel enjoyed the cozy living room where the wood stove had erased the chill of the October evening.

They invited Wisdom to join them. In the sweet silence, they waited to hear only from His Spirit.

This is what He said:

"For I know the plans I have for you," declares the King, "plans to prosper you and not to harm you, plans to give you hope and a future. Then you will call upon me and come and pray to me, and I will listen to you. You will seek me and find me when you seek me with all your heart. I will be found by you," declares the King.[20]

What did the future hold? Ariel wanted to serve Him with all her heart, yet carried a tremendous fear of failure. She was still healing from the torment of guilt from the destruction of her parents' marriage after the death of her brother Sammy. Those early hardships at home and school were firmly embedded in her inner self.

Ariel believed the future would be glorious, yet felt so fallible. Recently, a trial another girl from the village had undergone at a renowned college was weighing heavily on the community. Though receiving excellent marks, because of her convictions, her professors demanded she renounce the faith or lose the opportunity to receive her degree. She chose the King, and the College Board expelled her. In light of these things, Ariel wondered how she could do anything for Him without failing.

Ariel shared these concerns along with her recent experience of self-forgiveness with Ms. Jacqueline who prayed Ariel receive help regarding this delicate matter and be able to discern any traps of the Game Master. She told Arial she was confident the King desired her total freedom from oppression.

Then Ms. Jacqueline said, "Dear child, you are no longer living as a sinner saved by grace—that would mean you still have a lifestyle of sin. No, you are a saint who sometimes sins. Because of this complex world we live in, God's people fail and even sin, but He gave Himself to forgive us and make us whole. You are called to serve our glorious

---

20   Jeremiah 29:11-14. "LORD" changed to "King" for story purposes.

King, but how? Daily wait on Him and He will show you. He will never lead you astray or allow anything to occur which is not according to His plan, even unto death because He's got you. You belong to Him and that is your safety. You presently see your days as something you control. No, your days and times are in His hands. Because He is perfect, you can dwell forever secure with Him no matter what storm may be raging around you."

Ariel revealed to Ms. Jacqueline she was being drawn to serve the King in a distant land. Ariel became inspired by letters from His servants that were faithfully read to the congregation by her Shepherd. Many people didn't even know the King existed. Thus, they lived in harsh oppression from the Game Master, not realizing there was any escape. Ariel wanted to bring the King's message to people in remote places, opening the door of hope like those heroes of the faith. This was the first time Ariel had shared this dream with anyone. Late into the night they talked and prayed for the King's guidance.

Ariel surrendered her will to the King and prayed. Now she was safe in His arms, certain He would catch her lest she fall. Going up the stairs to her room, she wrote down the recent happenings in a love letter to the King. Soaring as on eagle's wings, she sent a kiss toward heaven, closed her eyes and sank into a blissful sleep.

Ariel began riding the mare to school instead of taking the ferryboat as before. When it was time, Fred would breed the mare with the stallion from the wild herd. Before long there would be a new foal on the farm.

There were other developments, Mom and Dad announced they were expecting a baby the following Christmas. Upon hearing the news, family and friends had a big celebration.

That next summer Ariel went on her first mission trip to a neighboring city. A group of young people from the church she attended were invited by a sister church to walk the city and pray for a week, then wait on Wisdom's instructions what to do next. Because this was a city well known for its strong faith, it seemed an unusual plan. Leaving the familiarity of her small village, Ariel was astonished by the tall buildings and fast pace. Churches of all sorts were practically on every corner. Many were grand, with beautiful stained glass windows and large groups of people streaming in and out.

Ms. Jacqueline, their leader, alerted them to the needs in the city. "They're naked and destitute," she told them. Though caught up in "holy activities," many weren't connecting their service to the Holy One. Division had developed from unproductive teaching among some of the congregations, thus keeping people blinded from the truth. "Not all accept the King," she warned. The King encouraged Ms. Jacqueline's group to teach about His character and truth rather than human interpretation. "Let My Spirit of Wisdom teach the people," He instructed.

Daily they waited for Him to lead in ways that would help this community. The young people were compelled to address differences that surfaced in their group, choosing to forgive and stand united rather than allow arguments to triumph. Thus they learned to overcome the Game Master's device of causing conflict among people. It seemed when the King's people magnified imagined slights toward each other to take hold, arguments and anger followed. Once they dealt with their own issues, the group thrived. From that point, when there were misunderstandings, they talked to the King and resolved them with one another. This foundation of love the King would soon have them share with others. As they firmly established themselves in His way, Wisdom gave steps to victory for this city that was so close to Him, yet so far.

After the week of prayer walking, Wisdom instructed them to write on pieces of paper personal messages from the Holy Book to be given to the people. That is exactly what the young people did. Soon, there were more than a thousand slips of paper. One young man was designated to stand on a crate in the city square and speak Words of Life, as the others prayed.

Once the message was over, they worshiped the King while a few of them gave the notes to people in the crowd. "If anyone wants prayer, come to the King in worship, and receive the Balm of Gilead poured out on your wounds and diseases," encouraged the leader.

By following Wisdom's direction, many people were united to the King. Years of misunderstanding melted away as the young speaker daily encouraged the crowd to receive truth: "Lay your burdens down at His feet, then forgive and reconcile with one another."

The people exclaimed, "What a Mighty King! We love Him. He is the One! Three in One, the only One. We must have Him." There was fresh anointing for every gathering as He healed the sick, saved the lost and restored broken lives. Those miraculous acts were just a few brushstrokes on His living masterpiece as they agreed to wait on Him. This experience increased Ariel's longing to participate with the King in setting captives of the Game Master free. Staying close to the King permitted her to witness blessings flow directly from His throne into the earth. Upon returning home, she eagerly started her last year in school preparing for the next assignment. Time went quickly, as Ariel stood at the threshold of promise to a life poured out serving the Love of her life.

After graduating, she went on a year Sabbatical to experience and prepare for the next great adventure. One of her favorite memories was swimming in tropical oceans with the whales. Ariel spent hours absorbing the healing sounds, listening to the massive sea creatures sing to one another. Mother to child, baby to father, mates young and old, joined until death. These magnificent sea creatures taught her what lasting relationships and healthy community were intended to be like. There were many species of creatures in the sea, and she never tired observing them. The complex rhythm of life in this magnificent creation intrigued her.

There were many lessons of commitment the creatures taught her from sea, land and air. It was human relationships that seemed so confusing. How could love create such pain? Why weren't her early childhood experiences as touching as these sea creatures' experiences seemed—although pain seemed to run deep for them, as well? Early each morning as the sun was cresting the dormant volcano, Ariel entered the water and listened to their songs.

Assembled one afternoon with other travelers overlooking the ocean at a gathering in the jungle, she witnessed a surprising sight. Fifty dolphins leaped out of the ocean in a salt-water ballet before their eyes. One jump, then down they plunged. After a few minutes, the travelers observed a couple young dolphins surface and follow the same dance, then quickly disappear into the ocean.

The travelers waited a long time, but they didn't resurface. Ariel continued to watch for them, ready at a moment's notice to be dazzled beyond comprehension in this amazing universe. Though still searching, she returned to the sleepy country town of her childhood.

After resting at the family farm, Ariel heard Wisdom's call while out riding the mare one afternoon. "You are ready. It is time for your next task." Ariel remained until camp meeting, going with her family and members of their small country church; for there were important lessons she must learn. Over the years, the members of the church had become very close, praying often for each other. Some of her friends were married with children of their own and either working their own farm or the family's homestead.

Ariel's brother, Simon, was already five years old. He brought delight to the family, almost completely erasing the loss of little Sammy. Her parents worked hard on their farm, and as a result were richly rewarded. Fred was now considered a valued member of the family. He spent tireless hours coaching Ariel how to train wild horses. She listened closely and learned much from him, for this skill could be valuable in the future. The King's ambassadors often traveled by horseback, and needed loyal steeds to do so.

"Have no fear," Fred told her, "In all you do, wherever you go, follow and obey the King. Be sure to accept and forgive your own little failures, and those of others."

"Choose your friends wisely," Ms. Jacqueline advised her, as they sat on a tree swing secured to a sturdy oak one day at camp meeting. "You shall experience tremendous joy and sorrow in this life. People need the King, they just don't know it. Remember, you are not the answer, He is. He will give you the words to say for each circumstance, you can always trust Him. Be His honest and humble vessel, even when you feel alone. Sometimes life seems like a little sailboat in the midst of a massive storm, keeling hard as the tip of the sail runs parallel to the sea. You may be hugging the line with all your might, hands bleeding and torn from the strain of the wind ripping the line from your hands. Keep your faith as the anchor in a mighty Rock. Speak to the storm and your soul, 'Peace, be still.' Though the storm may continue outside, you shall overcome as peace fills you within. Count on it, for the King is with you and will take you through anything."

The day before departing to the Land of Enchantment, Ariel went to visit her friend Vicky. Over the years, Vicky just became sweeter. Ariel admired her confidence and consistent kindness to everyone while living for the King. The two young women shared their memories, talking about yet unrealized dreams.

Vicki encouraged her friend saying, "Surrender daily to our precious Chief Shepherd, for there are many opportunities to go astray. Life is difficult for those who set themselves against Him and His people. The battle of whom or what masters us is intense and day-by-day choices determine our outcome. We can be easily distracted and respond to others out of brokenness, thus causing great harm. This is another device the Game Master uses to deceive us into acting out the seven deadly sins, which are a form of false worship. Surrendering daily protects us and when we do, the King shows us how to bring life to the perishing."

The two women reminded one another to be wary of wolves in the wild, and of men who masquerade as lambs. The two friends didn't want to leave each other's company knowing they would not see one another for a long time.

Before dark, Ariel rode back to her parent's farm. Mom had made her favorite dish for dinner and the family dined together by candlelight. Afterward, Dad brought out his fiddle with Fred on the harmonica as they danced to the cheerful music, worshiping the King well into the evening. Before going to sleep, the family anointed Ariel for the adventure that lay ahead. Ariel went to sleep listening to the gentle voice of the King within.

Chapter 18
At Sea

Ariel awaited the ferry with Dad, Mom and Simon the next morning that would take them to town. There she would board the train taking her to the East coast, then meet her ship heading to Africa. This whole journey would take a while.

Before leaving town, everyone prayed blessings and safety over her. Ariel's heart overflowed with encouragement and her eyes welled up with tears as she soaked in every word. She had only a small bag including a journal and the Holy Word. Many ladies from the church along with Vicky had prepared enough food to feed an army, doubling her load. Included was dry meat and gifts to give those she met along the way.

All too soon, the train whistle blew. The conductor cried, "All aboard." Ariel was helped up by an attendant's strong arm as the train slowly pulled away. The small crowd waved blessings and kisses to Ariel. Though no longer able to hear them, she read their lips, breathing life upon her until disappearing from sight.

Sitting down next to an elderly couple on the train, the gentleman commented, "You are very blessed, dear child, to experience so much love."

The three of them became fast friends, speaking of many things over their journey together. Her travel companions advised Ariel, "Remember, when you are alone and the cruel fingers of the Game Master seem to be grabbing you into his domain, do not fear. You are a daughter of the King who triumphs over every battle. In Him, you always war from victory, not for victory. Do not be deceived into thinking any task is too great or the circumstances too overwhelming, for He is the Master of war. Nothing is too hard for Him."

It turned out this elderly couple were representatives of the King heading back to the Australian Outback. The three of them rejoiced together in the One who brought abundant life. Ariel was infused with a fresh presence of the Spirit of Wisdom from the heavenly throne as the King spoke through that kind couple: "By wisdom a house is built, and through understanding it is established; through knowledge its rooms are filled with rare and beautiful treasures,"[21] the gentleman's wife quoted from the Holy Book.

Spirit, soul, and body, Ariel was that house being filled with eternal treasures. The counsel she received from the King was, "Stay close." That is exactly what she did. Too soon the three of them said a teary farewell, although Ariel promised to stay in contact by post. After they left, the King repeated, "Stay close to Me." This was to be her daily bread crossing the treacherous Atlantic in the days that followed.

Aboard the vessel were difficult days of terror for many passengers. Such would have been the case with Ariel, had she not trusted the King in advance. Never had she felt so close to death as when that old ship rode unending mile high waves. Once those harsh waves of the Atlantic hit, everyone went to their cabin overcome by sea sickness. In her despair, Ariel cried out and the King rescued her from even the fear of danger. Ariel was encouraged by one of the passengers to not eat meat or milk because the rough ride of the sea didn't allow good digestion for these strong foods.

Soon she was well enough to get out of her cabin. Ariel had learned an important survival skill: *When in unusual circumstances, reduce everything to its simplest form.* That truth she applied to many needs. Feeling better, she often read the Holy Word, wrote in her journal along with composing letters to her beloved parents. She mailed the letters at various ports of call after they crossed the ocean. She spent her time visiting other passengers who were still sick, both to encourage and pray for them.

One morning there was a lot of commotion topside. The crew was running back and forth on deck, as the Captain barked orders to prepare to dock at the first stop on the West coast of Africa

Once docked, the passengers disembarked, walking as drunkards from riding the wild waves. They had a few hours until departure

21   Proverbs 24:3-4.

while waiting for the crew to reload the vessel. Just as she learned from Ms. Jacqueline during high school, Ariel walked and prayed that territory accompanied by another lady she met on board. Most of the passengers were interested in trinkets, but not these two. They were committed to serve the King and didn't need to be bogged down with more stuff.

The passengers were overjoyed to hear the next part of the journey around the Horn of Africa through the Mediterranean would be tamer than the Atlantic. No longer seasick, they gathered as they had at the beginning of the voyage. Dinner parties and laughter filled the ship once again.

Ariel's anticipation was building as she came closer to her destination. This was the moment she was waiting on, and it seemed her whole life had led her here. The journey had given her plenty of time to reflect about this land with its many needs. She pondered some of the lessons already learned, such as the Game Master's lust-crazed sickness causing a person to do anything to get their needs met. That strange obsession left only destruction and damage in its wake. Her role was to work with others while heeding the King's instructions. Lives were in the balance, and as His servant she was thrilled to have been invited to partake in His miraculous interventions. All He required was that she listen ... and she was.

Chapter 19
Africa through Ariel's Eyes

Arriving at her destination, Ariel was met by a couple of young men, who took her where she was to be stationed. Here, instead of riding horses, the people rode huge elephants. Ariel was amazed at the sight. How would she describe them to her family and friends back home? Ariel asked the guides about them.

They told her, "Elephants are massive creatures that in the wild were free to live out their existence in peace. Many travelers desire the wealth attained by using them to transport illegal merchandise. Ivory poachers, slave runners ... let's not talk about such horrible things; yet they are a sad fact of life here."

"Some owners are good to their beasts of burden, using them only for necessary labor. Then there are those who are cruel to both their families and elephants. The gentle beasts are forced to carry loads of contraband as their owners traffic in activities such as stealing, running drugs, and trading illegal merchandise. That is how they get the name 'pirate elephants.'"

They went on to tell her, "Then there are the leopards captured for protection as well as companionship which offer both status and riches to their owners. To own one of these wild predators, you must be of a rare temperament, indeed. If they end up in the wrong hands, it can be disaster for everyone, including the owner—but you know how people are," one young man said. "Our natural tendency is to want what we want, when we want it, regardless."

Ariel recognized these evil practices brought to light the need people have for the King. Wanting to do our own thing is what got our ancestors kicked out of that perfect garden in the first place, she reflected. The Pandora's Box has been opened since to the Game Master to reign over us. This same lure he uses today. He leads us to believe we are in charge of our lives and can do or have anything we desire because we deserve it saying, "I am god!" Armed with that belief, the game is on. "What riches and treasures do I get?" The need then arises to harness creatures such as horses, leopards, elephants, sea cows ... along with man-made travel devices, to get stuff from here to there.

There is only one answer: surrender to the King. If the creature is captured by one who follows Him, great good is possible. But if the creature is captured by one under the spell of the Game Master, untold sorrow and devastation certainly occurs.

Ariel's curiosity about this amazing creation ran deep. She observed how some people want to understand everything that is going on in the world, experience both good and bad, and yet not get caught. This desire, once granted, becomes a painful sword usually not acknowledged until much later. Lust for self-satisfaction drives those who hold this view.

Ariel considered how obsessions brought pleasure to people as she traveled to exotic places around the world during that year after graduation. She had witnessed tropical "exploding" rainbows along the ocean's coast, then dog sleds racing across the tundra in the snowy slide. She had even met people who had traveled the jungles on actual pirate elephants for pirate traders and drug runners. She had seen astounding beauty next to overwhelming ugliness.

Some of what she had observed was beyond excruciating. All too often, many die as victims of the Game Master who lead them to depravity beyond comprehension because of lust for more. She knew Wisdom rescued people ensnared in pitfalls leading to death, having gotten too close to the edge on a few occasions while looking for *truth* embodied in love. If it weren't for the King, the Game Master would see to it that a person's weakness took control, and lead them into deadly paths. On one hand, Ariel was fearless, courageous, and capable. On the other she was alone and fragile, thus making her vulnerable to deception. Her weak point, the passion to help others, was also her greatest strength. Having witnessed many things in her travels along with experiencing miraculous restoration, Ariel desired to help others even more.

Blown about by love, fun and truth mingled in, she almost went over the edge, but Wisdom had mercy. She was destined to cross paths with a tremendous Warrior who would rescue her from aimless conquests. Led to the foot of the cross on more than one occasion, Ariel was on a mission to accomplish that end for not only herself, but for those willing to listen.

Chapter 20
Life in the Village

The little village she was sent to had experienced a lot of change over the years. Death, famine, disease, war, not to mention ongoing attacks initiated from power hungry men. Stealing children from peaceful villages was common. Raping, pillaging, and murdering adults, then burning down their homes, brought unbearable conditions in their wake. Children eating from garbage dumps, destitute, ransacked families the world over. People plundered and made to be slaves or even worse; entire communities made homeless by natural catastrophes such as earthquake, fire, or flood. Soon man-made catastrophes of disease arrived. Whole families were wiped out from war, AIDS, and famine, often leaving children under the care of just one surviving adult.

As awful as their situation was, those who escaped death often met worse peril. Food was scarce for war brought marauders that stole from the survivors leaving behind burned crops. In addition, the water had become so polluted it was almost like drinking refuse. All these elements together birthed malaria, typhoid, and the dreaded AIDS—a deadly cocktail the impoverished people were forced to drink. Die, or drink, and then probably die. The desire to live is very strong, so they drink.

Things had improved since the Doctor and his team arrived. They provided medical intervention while helping people restore the land, build irrigation canals and reroute waste water away from clean sources.

Ariel joined the team shortly after the orphanage was built. It seemed children came from nowhere. Though frightened and sickly, with the loving care of the Doctor and his team, many revived. News spread quickly throughout the region and crowds poured in, orphans beyond number. Other centers set up over the years attempted to fill the impossible need, but there still were not enough. Each adult cared for between ten to twenty children, and as they grew up, stayed to help the little ones-forgotten people, yet families to each other. Surviving adults came to the center and once strong enough, they remained to help.

Ariel joyfully immersed herself in the service of His people, speaking about the King continually. People learned the King was different from the oppressors they had been victim to, choosing to serve Him and delight in His ways.

Though financial support and medical supplies were sent to meet this important need from foreign places, it was often intercepted by war tyrants who built armies from children not fortunate enough to escape as the kids in the orphanage had. Ariel along with other adults lovingly cared for survivors who escaped unthinkable horrors. It brought great joy to watch their transformation as the King lifted them out of despair.

Over the years, Ariel assisted in training adults to start orphan homes in new villages. Soon she would leave with another team to start a new village of refuge. A couple new helpers were arriving by passenger freighter the next morning, bringing medical supplies and tents for the project. The location had been scouted out and deemed safe to start a new village. Ariel and her team would depart within a month.

Ariel went with three others to meet the new recruits. There was hard work ahead and the team held no notions of glamour about that fact. They needed to be encouraged in the training process, rather than be at odds because of romantic notions. Wisdom counseled them, "Time and experience reveal how much is truly unknown. Be humble and listen closely to the King. Without humility, people work out of their own ability and strength depleting the soul. Serving the King requires total dependence on Him, so don't hold back. Instead turn to Him as a supernatural response."

The newcomers needed to be taught the art of serving others as though serving the King. Because of the enormous needs, if performance rather than love were the focus, their strength would soon dry up. Unfortunately, when a worker left exhausted, the loss of that person was hard on the community. Too many had already left. Over the years the coordinators had learned to screen applicants well. Because they were responsible to provide the best for everyone, they learned to choose workers selected by the King who doesn't look at the outside, but the heart.

The team labored diligently to meet the needs of the orphans, working long hours and overcoming many obstacles. They sacrificed their own comfort for this labor of love, learning the King provides more than enough to satisfy every need.

Chapter 21
Made for Each Other

Ariel and Morgan answered the King's call and walked the path of the His choosing. Neither knew that with each footstep they were getting closer to experiencing the King's holy love ...

Ariel and her team went early to meet the new recruits arriving on the *Iron Mistress*. While excitedly discussing their plans, the ship's horn blew with fury as she pulled into dock and let down the gangplank. As the passengers disembarked, Morgan and Old Steward, filled with anticipation, followed them, no longer ship employees.

There were no crates for them to unload or plans to make for the next port of call. Just a few bags of personal items were all they needed to carry off the vessel. Cap'n Jack and the crew stood as honor guard for this unlikely pair passing to enter their next undertaking. Without fanfare they headed toward the station to meet the new crew.

When Morgan walked into the station, he gasped upon seeing her—Ariel, his bright light. Love as he never believed he would experience toward a woman flooded him. He knew in that instant they were made for each other.

He had never considered loving a woman, instead consumed with serving the King and His people. Meeting the needs of the brokenhearted, speaking Words of Life to the destitute, leading others to live within the kingdom of heaven on earth—those were his desires. But once he saw Ariel, something new was birthed within. He heard the King say, "This woman I formed for you to spend the rest of your lives together as soul mates. One day you shall be married and together accomplish what you never could alone. This is My will and My way. Follow Me in it."

Morgan's heart overflowed with love and contentment. Ariel was the woman the King had chosen for him. It seemed as though heaven opened and poured its contents into his heart. He fell completely in love, not able to take his eyes off her.

Introductions were made, but Morgan could hardly mutter hello. Following the team out of the station, Old Steward gave Morgan a nudge in his side, but the young man didn't seem to notice. He was reflecting on the young women he had met aboard the *Iron Mistress* who attempted to pursue him over the years. He hadn't been interested in frolicking with any of those beauties for his passion was the King's passion and none other.

But today, presented with his future bride, all the pieces of his life seemed to fit together—only he had no idea what to do with them. Walking through the bush, the rest of the group talked excitedly. Morgan remained silent, though, deep in thought, recognizing the King had carried him this far. *He'll cause Ariel to fall in love me.* Morgan was certain of that. This calmed his soul, causing all uncertainty to melt away. Morgan didn't need to force anything other than faithfully follow the King.

Reaching base camp that evening, Morgan and Old Steward retired directly to the men's quarters. Finally alone, Old Steward questioned Morgan about his unusual behavior.

Morgan replied, "Ariel is the one, I am certain. I am full of love beyond belief for her. The entire world cannot contain it; I am undone. Where I go, only heaven knows, but all shall be well as long as she is by my side."

Praying briefly before going to sleep, that night Morgan dreamed of the remarkable love from the King toward this intriguing woman. In his dream, Morgan saw himself standing in the midst of a holy fire speaking to people about the Kingdom of heaven. The cross boldly blazed behind him, or rather consumed him. Ariel was there praying as he spoke. The effect was overwhelming. People of all ages were calling for the King to come. Their faces represented various nations spanning the globe. One by one, they confessed faith in the King of heaven. This is what the King said to Morgan in his dream:

I have much I shall do in the days ahead, for you and My people the world over. I love My church and My people. When you avail yourself to My will, you see why. Isn't she beautiful? Isn't My church perfect in every way? Now you understand why I love her and long passionately after her. My ways are profound. I am calling My people back to Me. They are hungry for Me and My word. Your anointed call is to bring My message and My word. You needn't worry about the world and its ways. The world, the flesh and the Game Master are nothing compared to My Word.

I shall overpower all that stands in the way of My people hearing from Me. Beloved child, trust Me. I have many wonderful things to give you in the days ahead. Do you realize how precious you are to Me? How valuable a worker in My kingdom? Others cannot help but recognize My touch upon you. Do you? Open your eyes and your spirit completely to Me. You have never been a disappointment to Me. I love your open spirit, like that of a child. Keep coming deeper into My kingdom. I shall reveal how to accomplish the various tasks awaiting you. Enjoy the next phase ahead as My emissary. You are called and chosen.

Peace, My precious one. Enjoy the journey. Speak for Me. I anoint you and give you the words.

The King instructed Morgan to write down this message and share it with Old Steward, saying, "All these things shall surely come to pass, and I want you to remember I told you in advance what I shall do."

After sharing the dream, Old Steward told Morgan, "Though in this land these children are not from our earthly families, we can be as fathers to them. The heavenly Father helps us take care of them. He is all He says He is, and keeps all His promises, far beyond our comprehension."

The next morning the new recruits took a tour of the village. Though Old Steward and Morgan were newcomers to the region, they had been well schooled from their past and were ready to address the difficult issues before them. Both men were delighted at the opportunity to father others.

For Old Steward, this was a chance to make up for deserting his children as he and Morgan helped to restore the broken hearted. Since Morgan had been adopted into the King's heavenly family, he wanted to share this gift with others.

The King planted this desire in their hearts, for sorrow and painful losses are not to be wasted. Restored lives are part of the wonderful plans He has for all his children. Over that month, the team prepared while laboring together teaching the children, repairing homes and building sheds for the livestock to protect them from predators. Soon they would move to their new home.

Chapter 22
The Doctor Says Goodbye to His Children

Ariel had been up for hours attending to the needs in the village. She hated to leave this place, having a strong bond with everyone there, but the King was calling. This site was doing well. Still, there were reports of death and disease skyrocketing elsewhere. She surrendered her grief at leaving because of love for the King and His will. Since He was calling, it must be for the best. She spent her few remaining days in this beloved place with those who had become like family. It brought comfort that there were many hands to take care of the children when she left; besides, they would see one another again.

Preparing for the move, the new team gathered the necessities while learning to work and pray together. The Doctor who was leader of the community would take an assistant along with builders, a teacher, a farm expert, Ariel, Morgan, Old Steward and a few others. The team totaled a dozen people.

The Doctor had designed the village he was leaving named "Our Father's House." It had been founded on the Holy Word's instruction, which said, "A father to the fatherless, a defender of widows, is the King in his holy dwelling. The King sets the lonely in families, he leads forth the prisoners with singing; but the rebellious live in a sun-scorched land."[22] Having left worldly luxury behind over twenty years ago to build huts out of mud and dry grasses from the bush of Africa brought joy to his heart. Others called him crazy back then, but Wisdom just called him to obey.

Over the years the Doctor became like a parent to hundreds of deserted children left to die. He rescued many from untold horrors.

---

22   Psalms 68:5-6.

Their families had disintegrated, with only the elder children left to care as best they could for the younger ones. Often they had no hope.

Once Our Father's House was built there were clean water, schools, and abundant crops from the fertile fields nearby. As the children matured, they remained, becoming helpers to carry on the task of raising the younger ones. The new team would face trials ahead, but replicating the success of Our Father's House would avoid many difficulties. They would ask the King what to do next, and then follow Him—love in action. That is how previous orphanages the Doctor built succeeded. It was the most important thing they could do.

The new place they were going had undergone extensive destruction in the land among the people. This created overwhelming suffering, causing depression and anger in the people left behind. Their trust towards others had long ago disappeared. The young could only look forward to premature death for themselves and their elders.

The Doctor and his team knew the King reached past all torment by working through His people. Since his youth, the Doctor looked forward to bring complete healing to distant people and places. He chose the way of holy love when he accepted the call as a youngster after hearing about Moses' life story, the leader who said he wouldn't go another step unless the King accompanied him. The Doctor also needed the King's presence to be with him, like Moses in all he did while serving in unity with His people.

Though life in Africa was trying, the result had been worth it. There were many trials, but the Doctor learned patience in the process, even when others raised objections about the truth of the King's message. How did he determine to keep going? Seeing the human wreckage in others they asked, "What kind of love is this"? Having read the story they argued," Aren't we past this mess? Wasn't this foretold Savior going to rescue us and make everything perfect? Why are these horrible things still going on"?

From a human standpoint, addressing these questions with people over the years was tedious. Not for the Doctor and those like him. Rather, it was an honor to apply truth through the King's Spirit then watch supernatural transformation occur. The King repeatedly stepped in and breathed health into broken people while responding to their many concerns. When the Doctor was asked, "How?" he told them:

As the story goes, there was a man lying by the side of the road that had been beaten senseless. Left for dead, he lay there as many passed his way, but offered no help. Even upstanding citizens walked by and remarked, "Oh, a useless wanderer. He's of no concern to me." Whether fearful or disdainful, they would cross the street rather than get involved.

"Finally, an average sort of fellow walked past the suffering soul. Not thinking twice, he gently lifted the wounded man, put him on his donkey and took him to a nearby town. There he cared for the man, washing his wounds with wine to cleanse from infection because they were caked with blood and dirt. Afterward he applied oil to speed the healing process. Since he couldn't stay to care for the man, he requested the owner of the inn do so until the man recovered. He even committed to pay for any remaining charges upon his return."

The Doctor lived by this principle of selfless love in both word and deed, time and again bringing the wounded to the true Healer, for no one can heal or transform lives better than Him.

Taking this group of young people into unfamiliar territory, the Doctor wanted them to know He would be there in the dark night bringing solace and answers to their many questions. How could he provide what they needed? Recognizing his limitations, he asked the King to unfold His plan and give clear direction regarding the departure to the new village. Every detail was orchestrated by Wisdom and made clear by the Living Word. The necessary directions were revealed through the One who alone prepares the heart of the hearers.

The Doctor deliberately asked for Wisdom's intervention in everyone's presence, praying, "Keep ears and hearts focused on what you desire, binding all other distractions. Tell us Your message of truth alone and show us Your ways, O King, Amen."

Taking a deep breath, he surveyed the crowd. Everyone from the village assembled outdoors where nature seemed to be gloriously decorated just for them. Spontaneous praises to the King filled the village as the crowd worshiped Him. This brought another opportunity to receive healing as Wisdom poured in the oil and the wine, like the man in the story the Doctor told them about.

The people soaked in the experience as the sun shone in the brilliant blue sky that restful Sabbath day. Once they received all they needed they were ready to receive the message. Every eye and ear focused on the Doctor as he began to speak.

"Today, we have already met with the King. He heard our longing cries. Don't think He is done; no, He has just begun. As you know, this is our day to celebrate Him. Tomorrow our young trailblazers shall go further into the bush, offering their hearts and lives on the altar of loving service. There are many ready to hear the gospel of the heavenly Kingdom. Consider your own life as I read a story from the Holy Book in Genesis. Let's talk about an ancient Hebrew named Joseph."

The Doctor spoke of the many challenges Joseph had gone through. Starting with Joseph's youthful dreams and the coat of many colors that boasted he was father's favorite, he told of the brothers' subsequent resentment and revenge that almost led to murder. They choose to sell him and cover up the wicked secret, deceiving their father to believe his beloved son was dead.

"From there, Joseph went into slavery, experiencing both sexual harassment and false accusation of a rape from his owner's wife landing him in prison. The heavenly King's favor was on him and though a prisoner was promoted to oversee other inmates. Joseph was compassionate toward those suffering in prison and everything he did prospered. His integrity was evident to all," explained the Doctor. "When a couple new prisoners arrived, Joseph consoled them. They told their confusing dreams to Joseph who said the interpretation was not his, but that of the heavenly King."

The Doctor paused to challenge the crowd to think about how they respond to pain. "Do you honor your parents? Do you care and encourage those less fortunate than yourselves? In your "prison" experiences do you remain close to the King, or succumb to self-pity and complaints?"

He continued with the story.

"Then Egypt's Pharaoh, considered god of the land, had a strange dream; seven fat cows came to the river and ate skinny cows. Shortly afterward he had another dream that seven fat ears of corn ate seven ears of sickly corn. Pharaoh demanded an interpretation from his wise men but none could, for a negative significance to the dreams might cost their head.

"The Pharaoh's wine taster then remembered Joseph from prison as the reliable dream interpreter. Pharaoh ordered, 'Get him here now.' If it were me, after all Joseph had gone through, I would have lost hope of ever being set free. But that didn't seem to be the case, for when the key turned in the prison door; he quickly cleaned up and shaved before meeting with Pharaoh.

"Joseph boldly proclaimed the King of kings was the only true interpreter. What courage that must have taken! By that proclamation, Pharaoh, considered the highest authority, was informed there was One above him. Surely Joseph knew his life was at stake and could have been taken instantly. Refusing to compromise, instead he gave the heavenly King honor and majesty by clearly speaking only the truth.

"Joseph was rewarded and given second place of authority in Egypt. Life was protected for Egypt and many other nations during the seven year famine that followed, all because one man participated with the King of heaven."

When he was done speaking, the Doctor looked at the people he loved and said, "When you examine your walk in relation to this man of outstanding character, how is Wisdom tugging at your heart? Let us wait for Him to speak personally to each of us."

Then he sat down. Together they waited. First were the tears, followed by conversations with the King. The people encountered the King of Heaven who builds intimacy between us and Him. When they were ready, everyone prayed and anointed the team with oil. Words of Life poured hope like Living Water directly into their hearts. The people talked the remainder of the day about how they had experienced the supernatural. As for the team, they were prepared for the new assignment.

That evening the Doctor invited the team for a stroll while the sun cast her magnificent display, preparing to bow before the night sky. The path he led them on wound around a nearby stream. Before long, the buildings disappeared behind a veil of tall grass and wild flowers. As they walked, he pointed out how the people built this village with what was at hand. Combining mud and straw, they formed hard bricks that were attached to a framework of strong yet flexible branches. They designated buildings for the chapel, school, and the place they called home. The land was cultivated and the water rerouted to irrigate flourishing crops providing food for the people. Harvesting, hunting, fishing, and trapping provided ample nourishment where starvation previously reigned. They had built a hospital as the Doctor pointed out, for the people's needs were a priority.

When he first arrived, everything was a state of emergency. He had to decide how to meet the unending life-threatening needs far beyond his ability. He took one issue at a time: food, shelter, medical attention. The point he made to the team was though they may not know what was most pressing, the King did. The Doctor sought daily guidance for the people by taking Moses' example of leading the Israelites in the desert. Their freedom from oppression, hunger, and thirst were met by a daily supply of manna from heaven, an example that showed the Doctor how to distribute each day's portion to the people.

The Doctor told the team about his experience as a young man struggling at the university. At that time, the King had given direction through a dream about food. "I used to be consumed with watching my food intake, having a robust appetite that was starting to cause me trouble. I thought it would be nice to have manna from heaven, thus maintaining a proper weight. In my dream I saw the King's outline, though not the details of success. He was strong and powerful as He spoke to me about this manna from heaven. I was in awe; and I'd like to point out how great it felt talking to my Maker.

"Natural food so important in sustaining life the King likened to manna from heaven. He told me He wants to send manna from heaven for the people on earth. He put me in charge of this project. Just as Joseph helped his generation, I was to help this one not abuse their gift. Enchanted that He picked me to be part of this project, I awoke awestruck.

"I questioned others what they knew about manna. I knew this dream held an important message and was compelled to find out its meaning. Did you know *manna* in Hebrew means "portion"? To live in proper healthy portion regarding food is part of the meaning, but there is a deeper meaning the King wanted to reveal. Even now as I reflect back to my dream, I can see Him standing almost cloud-like, yet without details. Though a dream, it didn't feel like a dream. It seemed so real. You know, I was disappointed when I awoke. Certainly the King and I had been talking and He nominated me to be in charge of the manna to oversee the people not abuse it. The Bible story relates that storing extra makes it rot, and I was appointed to guard it and instruct the people how to treat it properly. Abba knows our nature of wanting more and never being satisfied.

"The lesson is this: He wants us to feast with Him daily, live by His rules and practice them. On the sixth day collect double, the seventh day is one of a Sabbath rest. This is difficult to do. I explain to people what is important for their well-being, but all too often they have their own idea about what is good for them. Their way is different than my dream and too often they do not accept the concept of portion.

"Rebelliousness hurts everyone, and knowing this causes me to be mindful of how I live as well as lead others. It was the dream of manna that taught me how to live long and be healthy. The memory of how little I was compared to our Creator is still very vivid. It was like seeing my unclear reflection through water when it ripples. He seemed all-consuming, yet I felt as safe as a baby in its mother's arms. In His presence I couldn't move; or could it have been a response to my awe of Him? I can't be sure, but it certainly was a great feeling of serenity, as though I was home.

"Strangely, the effect caused me to become more connected to reality and try to live His way consistently. I do my best to live by what I learned from a dream, and it shows in every aspect of my life. As for others, I keep trying to point the way. When they respond, I see awesome results. Do you understand what I am saying to you, or rather what the King is saying through me?" asked the Doctor.

Ariel was perplexed and asked the Doctor to explain further. "I am pleased you want to pursue this idea," he said. "In the beginning, I thought this vision was only about physical needs, but there is a much greater truth at hand.

"We as spiritual beings are having a human experience, not human beings having a spiritual experience. All too often, the challenges we are presented with create distance between us and our Creator. This separation is not how it was supposed to be-there is a bridge. Our King meets all our needs while steadily calling us to cross over that bridge with Him to one another. Since we usually eat daily to sustain our bodies, He speaks into our human understanding. Without food, we would get weak and eventually die. That is the ongoing problem we face here, especially in the bush. Long ago the earth was polluted because of the fall in the garden. We have been called out of that pit into the light. Our role as transformed people is to bring hope by planting crops, building homes and schools but especially teaching about the King.

"He desires to meet us and invite Him in as an act of our free will. He longs for us to do so. That is the main reason why we are here, to bring the truth. Spiritual food feeds our spiritual body, just as natural food feeds our natural body. He is the Bread of Life and as we feast on Him, we truly live. The battle may be difficult as you attempt to administer comfort to the lost. Even if all the resources were at your hand or you were the most powerful people on earth, which you are not, remember you actually have nothing to give. The battle belongs solely to the Master of War who is none other than the King. However, you may attempt to satisfy yourself or another, keep in mind only He possesses that ability.

"He owns the cattle on a thousand hills. If you are hungry, He will butcher a cow. If you need resources, He will sell one to provide for your needs. Whatever He says, it happens. There is no one like Him for He is the true Manna. We continue to mature by trusting Him completely as the one who provides all our needs.

"I am giving you sound advice. Set aside time daily to break bread with the King of kings. He is the answer. I am aware this experience is personal, one to diligently pursue. Surely pruning will come but rejoice, the fruit shall be delectable, bringing nourishing life wherever you go. Just remember He is the Provider, not you.

"This concept is difficult to accept. I suppose that is why He gives us the lesson of manna. For years, my life was about supply and demand; money, food, resources even speaking the right word. It took the fiery furnace of attempting to fix others that broke me, showing this deeper spiritual meaning. I am telling you this hoping the price I paid to learn these lessons will hasten your freedom. Encourage one another while holding each to account in love.

"I bless you with strength, unity, and joy. May everything you do bring healing from the King of heaven. Enjoy the process resting in the assurance that with Him even the darkest night is bright. Let me emphasize again, nothing is too hard for our King."

By now the stars had appeared and were glistening like millions of heavenly diamonds decorating the sky. The Doctor encouraged them to look up and quietly reflect as together they communed with the King.

Morgan became even more determined to win Ariel as his bride, recognizing her commitment to the King. She was the one for him, he was certain. As he lay on the cool grass looking up to the heavens he petitioned the King, "Show me Your will and confirm the cry of my heart. If this is the woman You made for me, will you cause our love to grow and last our entire lifetime? In Your Holy Word You say, 'What the King has joined together let no man tear apart.' If this is Your intent, cause her heart to be drawn toward me, and join us forever as one."

The King responded, "You are both in My hands. Follow Me in the way I reveal, and you shall end up at My desired destination. As we journey together, you shall experience abundance for I Am your contentment."

Underneath the heavenly canopy, Ariel and the King were having their own intimate conversation about Morgan. He pointed out to her very clearly, "This man is My choice for you. Together you shall do what you could never have done alone."

What a mighty King.

Chapter 23
Greenwater

"Nicer far when there are two. There are many little pleasures, when all is said and done—

For those who care to take them. But it's lonesome-like alone—so shall we take life ... together?

For it's always nicer far when there are two."[23]

As time passed, Morgan successfully wooed Ariel as they worked side by side, once they arrived at the new place. She eventually fell in love with him. After the King confirmed His will and Ariel was sure within herself, she and Morgan were married in the Land of Enchantment. Together they served the King there until it became clear they needed rest apart from others.

Morgan and Ariel were directed to a place called Greenwater by Aleah, a follower of Wisdom. Aleah found this place and recommended they go there. Later they thought back to their introduction to Greenwater and realized they had no idea how greatly it would impact their future.

Upon hearing the name Greenwater they couldn't help but wonder where the name came from. What caused it to be green? Green was an unusual color for mountain water. Was it infested with algae? Was it stagnant? Positive the best water is crystal clear, thinking it might be impure, almost prevented them from going. But Aleah was insistent they would love it, so up the mountain they went.

A gatekeeper at the entrance to Greenwater met them, recommending they purchase a pass to not suffer loss from the authorities. Having little money, Morgan and Ariel looked at each other with uncertainty.

"Is he worried about us, or just greedy?" Ariel remarked.

"I don't know," Morgan admitted

They went ahead and bought the pass, though later realizing they didn't need one. Rather than attempt to analyze the gatekeeper's intent, they chose to pray and commit him to the care of the King. They knew that was the kindest thing they could do, rather than allow a bitter root of resentment to form against him. As they walked further into this remote place, they could tell they were going in the right direction by recognizing the landmarks Aleah had told them about.

Exactly as Aleah instructed, they went all the way to the Threshold of Change, where pirate elephants gathered. That's when they realized that the gatekeeper had only been concerned for their safety, for he knew of the dangers there.

"Perhaps the gatekeeper didn't want us to spook the elephants and get trampled by them and their riders," Morgan guessed as Ariel nodded agreement.

Forgiving the gatekeeper of bad intent, they repented of their unfair evaluation and focused on finding a place to camp. They wanted the place Wisdom selected, for they sought to commune with the King and one another.

From previous experience they knew they must get all they could from the lessons Wisdom wanted to teach here. After a bit of exploration they found the spot. It was not pristine as they hoped, for it had been desecrated by pirate elephants and their riders. Garbage scattered everywhere gave evidence the riders had been drawn to Wisdom, but instead chose to worship entertainment provided by the Game Master.

Before Morgan and Ariel set up camp, they cleaned the place up. Round the camp they went, removing waste from pirate plunder. Satisfied, they invited Wisdom to fill this place and meet with them while safely resting in His presence.

Morgan and Ariel set up camp on the bank of Greenwater. They situated their chairs a few feet from the river's edge, starting a fire to heat the water for mid-afternoon tea. Waiting in the stillness of the forest, they gazed upon the living masterpiece.

In this remote place far from the hubbub of the city were no man created sounds, only raw beauty shared in the wilderness with their Beloved. It took a few hours of quiet meditation before their brains could engage in Wisdom's flow. It was necessary to rest, for they had been working hard for a long time in the King's field.

They were encouraged yet saddened with various emotions. During their time of reflection they recognized how powerful their choice to heed the voice of Wisdom versus the Game Master had been. Matching pieces together brought many memories to flash through their mind. Because their brains were clearer, they had insight how these voices had affected their life. Their thought process became more reliable and the relationship with Wisdom grew stronger as a result. Becoming keenly aware how the tricks of the Game Master were used to bring harm, they vowed to avoid them at all cost.

In the beginning, their brains soaked up the healing nature and intense beauty of this place. Surprisingly, Greenwater was not stagnant, but rather very much alive. The effervescent blue-green in the deeper pools gave the effect of Living Water that sang as the river rushed by with its babbling sounds. The water splashed over the rocks going down the mountain to join its destination elsewhere, permeating their inner beings with life.

In the middle of the pool was a tree trunk about six feet tall and six feet in circumference. For generations it must have thrived in the water until the tree broke, possibly from a heavy storm. Healthy baby trees now grew out of its peat mossy top, as the remaining trunk corroded. Looking inside, there appeared to be a tunnel-like entrance that disappeared into an unseen place. Around the trunk previous travelers had made a rock dam supported by the tree roots, forming a pool deep enough to swim in. Water flowed over the carefully placed rocks and allowed just the right stillness mingled with soft movement to draw Morgan and Ariel into deeper reflection. "Deep calleth unto deep at the noise of thy waterspouts,"[24] Ariel whispered.

As the water danced by, Morgan and his wife talked about the impact of the Game Master upon travelers such as the pirates—had they been drawn here by Wisdom? He invites us all to communion,

24   Psalm 42:7.

but did the rush to fill other longings cause them to choose the intoxication of the plunder they attained? It seems the choice to be submerged in "the world, the flesh, and the devil" powerfully turns people further away from Wisdom.

"The Game Master lures so many by his ever elusive promises. No one is immune to his temptations," said Morgan.

Ariel agreed. "This is not unique at all. We've seen the devastation happen in our short lifetime repeatedly."

They talked about how they had seen others make many wrong choices. The lures to pursue that way were as varied as the colors in a peacock feather, but the intent was always the same. The Game Master used every means necessary to distract people away from Wisdom's call and purpose. He promises fulfillment to travelers as long as they do as commanded. That free choice from an individual is required to produce either destruction or liberation. A person's true power resides in free will, they agreed.

Together they came up with a simple outline of the process: At a certain age, usually during the early years, an individual experiences a hurt beyond control that is often secretly orchestrated by the Game Master. He then presents himself as the perfect solution to an imperfect situation. An attitude then forms that is contrary to the healthy maturity of the individual. This strategy: Crush, build, lure, entice, crush—occurs over and over until bitter attitudes become natural to the person who invited them in. Those distractions from pain initially bring peace. Tasting this fruit temporarily offers satisfaction to the appetite bitterness demands. Soon the unwary person partakes again and again. The obsession continues even after learning about the deadly side effects.

"When the next difficulty inevitably came, the Game Master reminds them how favorable the previous outcome had been; how following him caused the pain to go away," Ariel commented. "Soon the individual easily repeats these behaviors, becoming less influenced by their conscience."

"Yes, and with that repetition, in time a habit is formed," replied Morgan.

It then becomes an automatic response: if this pain, then this response. The response, now a repeated one, could be food, drugs, sex, or a host of other abuses. Other behaviors associated with following the Game Master can include socially acceptable choices such as education, attainment of wealth, shopping, or climbing the ladder of success.The possibilities are endless.

The ultimate goal is to deaden resistance from the person's conscience. Once successful, the person can continue engaging in any or all of these possibilities without remorse. Once the deadening is complete, the individual fully becomes the property of the Game Master, subject to his cruel whims. Often he uses these individuals to lure inexperienced travelers into these behaviors promising satisfaction, thus drawing endless victims into the vortex of confusion.

Yet Wisdom is always there, waiting. Just as Wisdom had waited for Morgan and Ariel, he desires the affections of every traveler.

During the beginning of their stay at Greenwater, they focused on the impact of the Game Master. They felt his eerie presence while looking at the trunk of the broken tree, supposing imps and trolls dwelt there. They even imagined a gremlin hiding in the rotted-out center of the tree trunk. Though not believing he could harm them, they acknowledged how others could be lured by the Game Master and his aids.

As joined travelers, Morgan and Ariel were drawn to people trapped by life controlling habits, and they desired to reveal the path to freedom. This was their main reason to be here, for the King had actually invited them to rest and commune with Him. He said, "Come unto me, all you who are weary and burdened, and I will give you rest. Take my yoke upon you and learn from me, for I am gentle and humble in heart, and you will find rest for your souls. For my yoke is easy and my burden is light."[25] Realizing the Game Master couldn't harm them any longer, they entered the presence of their Beloved Creator.

The Lover of souls was free to lead them into His embrace with instructions of what lay ahead; His love is our true home.

---

25   (Matthew 11:28-29).

Part IV
Todd, Tony, and Francoise

Chapter 24
The Game and the Players

Save me, O King, for the waters have come up to my neck. I sink in the miry depths, where there is no foothold. I have come into the deep waters; the floods engulf me. I am worn out calling for help; my throat is parched. My eyes fail, looking for my King. Those who hate me without reason outnumber the hairs of my head; many are my enemies without cause, those who seek to destroy me. I am forced to restore what I did not steal. You know my folly, O King; my guilt is not hidden from you.

(Psalm 69:1-5)[26]

They were three friends who had known each other practically since birth. They had many memories over the years from their experiences together. Some were great, like the time Francois turned twelve at that birthday party his mom had for him.

All his friends were there, about ten boys swinging at a piñata hanging from an apple tree that had started blooming in the back yard. It was one of those perfect spring days. The sun was warm as the glistening light dappled through the new leaves on the trees. There was a sweet smell of fresh cut grass from the neighboring lawn. The boys were wildly swinging a bat (as only boys can do), to break the piñata for the candy inside. Crash! Out spilled the candy. It was Tony who rescued them from waiting any longer. As usual the victor and conqueror, this time it was the piñata. Wow, that was fun. Of course, François's dad didn't show up, which was standard. Mom was acting giddy with her ever-present glass of wine. Dad was not around much anymore, maybe because of mom's stack of empty bottles—an educated guess, thought Fran-

---

26   Changed "God" to "King" in this passage for story purposes without changing the meaning of the verse.

cois. That was the last day, he vowed, he would wait for his dad. And so it was.

Now that he was seventeen, his dad was trying to edge in since Francois had become somewhat of a star on the basketball team. His two best friends on earth, Tony and Todd, were also on the team, making it a perfect season. The three of them were stars in school with good grades and, of course, plenty of beautiful girls pursuing them. Colleges were knocking down their doors, too; these boys would be a prize to any institution.

Francois hadn't heard from his dad much since he turned fourteen, seeing him maybe four or five times since the divorce. But now, his dad said he found "religion" and its leader was called the King. Francois didn't care, besides his dad had been responsible for plenty of broken dreams from the broken promises he hadn't lived up to. How was this King guy going to make him any different, anyhow? There was no more room for a dad in his life, Francois was nobody's fool. He wasn't about to open the door and be met with rejection ever again.

So that was it and the door remained slammed shut. Now it was his turn to break promises. His dad showed up to his games all senior year, then graduation, but it was already too late for his son. The bleachers were open to the public, and his dad was just one of the public as far as Francois was concerned.

Francois' goal was stardom. College, pro ball, beautiful wife, smart children, fancy house with a swimming pool and feelin' easy summertime all year around. Money would be no object, for it would flow in like water over the Niagara, of that Francois was sure. Don't forget the great car; a Mercedes, no, a Porsche, no, a limo with a driver... Wait, all of them. He would have plenty of money to spare, plus throw in a sports car or two, a yacht ... his endless dreams were very attainable, considering his talent.

He would pick his college by what it would do to help him fulfill those dreams. Of course there was the summer adventure right after high school graduation. He and his buddies had already made an agreement years ago, and that was a sure promise. The tickets had been purchased and plans were made—everything was set.

Their relationship was very deep considering how different their personalities were. Tony was the tough one of the bunch. He grew up fighting his way through life. Some said he had a chip on his shoulder, but he didn't care about what people said. The point was that he had found a way to direct his aggression. Besides, there was no need to investigate those broken places. His parents were married, but unlike Francois' mom, Tony's mom was sweet, although quiet and distant. His dad, well, let's put it this way, Tony envied Francois that his dad had left. At least for his friend there weren't the other abuses or desertions Tony endured.

Tony didn't think much about that kind of stuff. He was just tough in his cool, harsh way. Good thing sports and his buddies were there for him. That's what kept him out of juvenile detention on more than one occasion. At one point he considered joining a gang, but his friends didn't want to so that got played out pretty quickly. Besides, they were family enough for him.

He was ready for college ball, but first, summer. Since their days together as boys they had agreed on it. There was a starting point to "the adventure." It was like a treasure hunt with instructions they drew up to follow, such as "look here." Then, "eat this" ... "great view" ... "park here" ... "try this." They would sample everything they wanted to along the way.

They had help drawing up the plan from a secret entity called the Game Master. He defined the plays and moves like their coach, but the end result promised *fun*. They first met the Game Master during an Ouija board game that had been given to Tony. In time they discovered how to access him easily without it and like many of their friends had grown accustomed to his alluring voice and ways. They gladly followed him at gatherings, enjoying the rewards they received from him.

They dreamed of the day to play "the summer game" and the promise of adventure and excitement accompanied by bright lights and sensations, along with much more. Look at them now—college, sports, too cool, and too smooth. That Game Master took good care of them, pointing only to a clear path shining ahead.

Then there was Todd. He had it made. Loving parents, money, along with a gorgeous sister, who wouldn't be happy being him? His mother asked him, "Why do you choose such complicated friends?" He couldn't explain it to himself, yet their camaraderie meant the world to him.

When he was a toddler, he was a cranky child, always crying. One day his mom tried to cheer him up, so she took him to a toy store. As he yelled, a lady approached them in the store and said to his mom, "You are so lucky to have a bad baby, things can only improve."

Well, they had for Todd matured into a very content young man. He was the anchor of the three, keeping them from going too far out. Soon they would fulfill their mutual dream. It was only a couple more months and summer would be here. They attempted to wait patiently for that day.

"We won! State champions! College of our choice, the three of us together ... graduation!" they shouted when they won the state finals.

Todd and Tony counseled their friend, "Francois, you have to leave that girl of yours. She is a chain around your neck. We have plans, futures filled with only good times, besides, remember the Game Master. Everything has already been mapped out, and she doesn't fit into the lineup. Plus, she isn't giving you what you want—one of those good, churchy-like girls. What are you thinking! Sure she's cute, but she is a ball and chain holding you back. Wait until after college then decide if she fits into your lifestyle. You know the saying: 'If you have something, let it go. If it comes back to you, it is yours, if it doesn't, it never was.' Well, right now, she is that something standing in our way. *Let her go*!"

Chapter 25
A Dangerous Woman

The young men's farewell party was fantastic. Family and friends celebrated at the catered event that had been lavishly provided by Todd's parents. They held nothing held back for the young men of promise.

The next day they would depart beginning the two-month adventure they had anticipated practically their whole life. They earned money through odd jobs along with gifts from family members and their allowances to provide for their needs. The adventure had begun.

The party went well into the night, with no restrictions. It should have been a memorable event, but unfortunately, they were too foggy to remember much of anything the next morning. Francois said goodbye to his girlfriend Lizzy, although not completely breaking up with her at the airport, and off they went. Todd held the original map in his hand along with a revised version. As the three of them put their foot on that plane, they waved goodbye to the world they used to know.

The first stop was Adult Disneyland, the place their childhood officially ended. The Game Master launched them off with a bang. As far as they were concerned, there were only happy trails ahead. This place was exciting; with so much to see and do there was no way to take it all in. Fast and furious, they careened wholeheartedly into the game. No stake was too high, no taste prohibited. Besides, no one was reading their mail and they were adults now, free to do as they wished.

After a few days, they boarded the Super Colossal Roller Coaster spanning the bridge between sanity and insanity. The sign posted on the arch to entrance of the station stated, "Welcome, your journey begins here." They were ready, fueled up on joy juice and an intense anticipation that had been building over their last few days' activities.

Carrying "guy stuff" in their backpacks, they stood in a long line, with a short wait. There were a few nervous giggles and muffled questions in the crowd like, "Have you been on this before? What is it like? What happens and how will it affect us?" Other than that, the crowd waited quietly, most of them with a glazed look in their eyes.

Out of nowhere, it appeared and everyone got on. There were people seated aboard with the seats tilted back in lounge style. They couldn't see the passing terrain, only the sky and horizon because the windows were situated up too high. Their height was a safety feature, for if they could actually see how fast they were going, the blur would have made them dizzy.

Once everyone was seated, the Coaster slowly started up, and then whoosh! That frenzied, insane, fast, up-down, ultra-crazy sensation hit. Periodically, it would stop at key places around the globe for people to get off and on, but overall, no one talked when the train was in motion. Mesmerized by the experience, there was nothing left to say.

The guys arrived at their first destination somewhere in China and stumbled off, excitedly telling each other about their wild experiences aboard the Coaster. Wandering around the city a few days, they were offered many things by the natives, who considered them "rich foreigners." Their senses were overloaded. Though wanting to try everything, the samples became too heady to continue.

All too soon, it was time to depart. Walking through the complex maze of the city, they arrived at a bus station. Their bus had tinted windows to see out, but not in. Once boarded, the three friends sat next to the driver, a Game Master guide. It didn't take long to understand that his ways were sinister. "Game Guide," as he liked to be called, spoke strange things to the travelers who listened intently to him the whole time. The bus passed through bizarre terrain of gnarled trees and bog land that wound around into a series of dangerous tunnels. The whole way, the guide said evil things, but everyone appeared comfortable in this strange "normal."

Upon reaching their destination, the bus pulled up next to a large home-style hotel where a smooth-speaking host greeted them. As he spoke, Todd thought he saw two guests devoured by hideous beasts. It was quick, like a flash of light. "No, can't be." Todd told himself he must just be over-tired or hallucinating. Besides, no one else seemed rattled. Meanwhile, the host didn't skip a beat as he spoke to the crowd.

After everyone had eaten their meal, the guys went to their room on the second floor right next to a grand winding staircase. Tired from the trip and appreciating the quiet, they immediately fell asleep. The next morning they awoke to the delicious smell of home-cured bacon and hurried downstairs to the dining room and ate with gusto.

As they were about to leave, Francois looked up the spiral staircase by the door and saw a beautiful woman walking toward him. He was drawn to her like a magnet. Though he sensed something seemed evil about her, his desire overcame any discomfort and he quickly shook off the feeling. She put out her hand for him to take to his lips, introducing herself as DeShellia. Her name was as silky soft and alluring as her hands, her face was absolutely lovely. He immediately became her captive. After introductions, they lingered in the library next to the staircase. Her speech tugged at his secret fears and desires. At first her power had little effect on him, which she must have noticed because she toned down her approach after a while—but her persuasive words began to get inside Francoise' soul.

Francois couldn't stop thinking. *I'm very attracted to her. Should that frighten me?* He understood why his buddies had encouraged him to leave his beloved Lizzy. She couldn't hold a candle to this breathtaking creature. Not only was she beautiful, she possessed qualities that would cause his professional basketball career to explode. The way she moved and her demure looks had the effect of enticing him into incredible longing. He imagined her showing up at celebration parties or accompanying him to engagements, the media would love her; she would be his queen.

All these thoughts came to him while taking in her every curve. She filled him with an excitement he had only dreamed about. When she spoke, her words sounded soft and sensual to his ears, adding to the already heightened energy between them. He had known many women, but she quickly wrapped him up in a seductive spell.

Todd and Tony knew their friend—once Francois was interested in a woman, there was no sense attempting to wait for him, so they left. They had their own pleasure to pursue, picking up a few souvenirs while sauntering around town. "He has totally forgotten us by this time," Todd said to Tony, as they both snickered.

Francois was now free to ask DeShellia to show him around the sprawling hotel grounds. He suspected the place was not called "The Palace" by mistake. When Francois offered his arm, DeShellia put her delicate arm in his and off they went two very vibrant young adults.

Having lived by The Palace her whole life, DeShellia told Francoise she was quite familiar with the area. With that seductive voice, she started to tell him about her hopes, dreams, and wishes. They walked along the grounds, passing the pasture where horses were running, their healthy coats reflecting the warm summer sun.

First the pair headed toward the greenhouse; Francois was interested in seeing the rare flowers inside. He was glad he said goodbye to Lizzy in his mind. Now he was free to be the man he wanted to—and DeShellia made him feel like that kind of man. Her touch, her words, though unusual at times, triggered hidden needs that had been overlooked as he was growing up. We're totally into each other, he realized, unlike the way my mom and dad behaved before he left.

Before they divorced, the drinking and arguing went on constantly. Their house was never inviting; rather, it was a place of turmoil. As a child needing the attention and love of his parents, Francois heard only slamming doors and harsh words. The most painful comments of the two adults preoccupied with their troubles were, "Leave me alone Francois, I am too busy for you right now." The good days were when they were gone, Mom to her room in a drunken stupor and Dad out chasing some fantasy.

The first time he received attention from a girl was in the fourth or fifth grade, he couldn't quite remember. Once he ogled some grownup pictures at a friend's house and from then on, he experienced relief from pain through sexual expression. The cycle that had started when he was young soon wore a deep groove in his need to escape the pain of reality.

Yes, he was glad Lizzy was far behind. It would have been boring to travel and have to miss all the excitement. Lizzy wanted monogamy, a family—the King's goals she told him. DeShellia at this moment fascinated him—her touch, the fantasy of excitement. She provided that and seemed to promise even more.

They entered the mysterious greenhouse, a virtual Garden of Eden filled with exotic plants Francois never knew existed. Arm in arm he and DeShellia walked, pausing before a brightly colored orchid here or an extravagant display of tropical greenery there. The huge greenhouse had many mini-gardens with private resting places built within the foliage.

The young couple sat down to rest by a fishpond with a small waterfall, enjoying the experience. Francois told DeShellia of his career waiting after college, as she quietly listened. Occasionally she lowered her long eyelashes and then reopened those large green eyes, giving him a captivating smile. He was hooked.

Sometimes she said alarming things that enticed him even more. Though he obviously desired her passionately, she kept him at arm's length. Needing to let off some steam, he invited her to join him for a horseback ride. As they were leaving, a man walked by and spoke to them. In the interchange, Francois had the unsettling sense DeShellia knew him a little too well.

Going to the stable, they asked the groom to saddle up the horses, as he questioned Francois about his riding ability. The groom told Francois, "DeShellia is an expert rider and has ridden frequently. Can you keep up?"

He gave DeShellia the frisky mare and after learning Francois was an accomplished rider, the groom gave him a strong steed in need of a hard gallop. They rode toward the neighboring fields that led into the woods and miles of trails.Once mounted, they headed into the surrounding countryside that went on seemingly forever. Not without notice, this striking couple raced their energetic horses.

Then the terrain changed, becoming dense inside the bamboo forest with trails winding around the hills into the mountains.

They rode through the lowlands where farmers in the area worked both rice and poppy fields. The poppies supplied opium in substantial amounts. DeShellia told him the drug was highly addictive. The good income received from opium sales was usually squandered on a lifestyle dedicated to its use. Some rice farmers attempted to create a different environment for their families and communities, but the drug business had such a great impact that many eventually lost their children to that trade. DeShellia was well acquainted with how the business worked being a daughter of an opium farmer.

She told Francois they would be riding past the back part of her father's fields toward the bamboo forest on a trail leading to a small Buddhist monastery. Since it was getting close to lunchtime, DeShellia told Francoise, "I know of a quiet spot to enjoy our lunch, it's a perfect distance from inquiring eyes and minds of neighboring residents and those at The Palace."

Riding through the forest, DeShellia looked approvingly at Francois's athletic body. She was well-known for making fast friends with attractive male guests of The Palace. Obviously, Francois is a catch, she told herself. Handsome, strong, a wealthy and virile American. How she could benefit from him was limitless.

She had acquired plenty of young men's hearts and gifts as personal trophies. She cared little that she had a reputation of consorting with the guests, but took pleasure getting what she wanted from them. Once she got bored or their resources were exhausted, whichever came first, she dropped them. She mulled over her plan of finding a wealthy man to take her away from this life. Maybe Francois was that man.

❖ ❖ ❖

As for Francois, his thoughts were of a different nature. That was why he appreciated running those powerful horses. He hoped to meet those needs soon, maybe during the picnic lunch. DeShellia slowed her mare to a walk in order to cool the horses down before stopping. Passing the monastery, she didn't want to bring dishonor to the gods or the monks as they rode by.

Francois had never seen a monastery before and thoughtfully considered both its grandeur and simplicity. He watched the monks going quietly about their tasks, working the grounds where the scent of incense was strong. The gardens were perfectly kept on both sides of the path leading to a statue of an enormous golden Buddha located by the large double door to the temple. The mountains and forest in the background gave a tranquil look to the place.

Looking at the temple reminded Francois of a letter his dad sent him before leaving home. It actually was a warning to keep from idols and only serve the One True King. As far as Francois was concerned, this King business was all a hoax that was fabricated to control the masses and keep the general population from total anarchy. He had no opinion about that Buddha or the King. It all seemed like foolishness to him.

He was on the adventure of his life, and nothing was about to get in the way of the good times ahead. People who held these types of beliefs had nothing but restrictions in regards to serving any spiritual entity—that was why he followed the Game Master. No rules— only permissiveness.

Up ahead was a little clearing in the woods where a log had fallen that they could sit on and enjoy lunch. DeShellia always loved this place. As a child, she came here with her Daddy before things changed. Those were good memories. That's when her Mommy was still alive, and though poor, they were a happy family—she, her parents, and two brothers.

Daddy used to tell her about the monks and how they had taken a code of silence to serve the big gold Buddha. Intrigued, she chose to worship the statue, but silence was all she received. When Mommy attempted to give birth to her last child that is when everything changed. DeShellia learned to live the way of quiet. As her baby sister was being brought into the world, her Mommy poured hers out, leaving them forever.

This crushed Daddy, leaving him a broken man; the love of his life was gone. There were no more words, only the opium pipe that soon appeared. Somehow her older brothers started a small opium farm, and Daddy just evaporated in billows of smoke steadily surrounding him. DeShellia was left to care for the baby, and the whole house fell into the unbearable trance of quiet. No laughter, no tears or words, only survival ... and opium.

DeShellia learned to use her wits and beauty to get what she wanted. Having no need for love, for it brought nothing but disappointment; she learned what was valuable from opium retailers who came to buy stock from her brothers. She had what it took to entice a man, satisfy him, and eventually get what she wanted. As a child, men gave her candy and little toys. But as a woman, well, she had much greater needs. Sex was her means to that end.

As she set out their lunch, DeShellia used her charms to bring Francois into her domain. She wouldn't give up anything without getting all she wanted. Demurely, she enticed him enough to keep him pliable in her grip. After lunch, it was time to return to The Palace for the afternoon party. By this point, Francois was willing to do anything she wanted, so long as he could experience her touch.

As they mounted their horses, she ran ahead, challenging Francois to a race back to the hotel. Both of them were involved in their own thoughts as they galloped back. Francois was used to women falling all over him, but DeShellia was different. He sure was enjoying this game with her while challenging himself how long it would take before he could wear her down.

They noticed a crowd gathered at the Palace's grounds. The afternoon party was in full swing, a favorite event among the guests and community. Groups of people were seated outside in the specialty gardens. On the front porch about twenty individuals were chatting casually, sipping their afternoon drinks.

Once Francois and DeShellia returned the horses to the care-taker, DeShellia told him she would rejoin him in a few days, for she must first attend to urgent business. Before walking away, DeShellia put out her petite hand for him to gather into his and gently kiss. She then headed toward the greenhouse and quickly disappeared. He watched to see if she would return, but she did not. Though puzzled, he looked forward to seeing her again, and maybe then he would have his way. Until then, he would enjoy The Palace experience.

Francois slowly walked back to his room to clean up after the lusty ride. Seeing Todd and Tony on the porch, he told them he would return shortly. After he left, Todd and Tony placed bets on what had happened between him and DeShellia. Though she appeared mysterious and exciting, they had seen their friend with girls before. They agreed his revolving door would probably keep turning for a long time.

Two are better than one, because they have a good return for their work: if one falls down, his friend can help him up. But pity the man who falls and has no one to help him up ... Though one may be overpowered, two can defend themselves. A cord of three strands is not quickly broken.[27]

"Guess he'll fill us in, but she looks like trouble to me," Todd said. "Do you remember our senior year, when ... ?" The two friends were happily recounting the high school scene until Francois returned. They kept on talking as vivid memories filled their minds throughout the afternoon.

As for the bet regarding DeShellia, Todd won yet again. He was usually good at reading people. She seemed like the cool, distant type, and though he hadn't spoken to her, he had a bad feeling about this girl. Tony and Francois respected Todd's ability to identify difficult situations and people. Not being one to keep his opinion to himself, he gave Francois a brisk shake on the arm and made clear this girl was to be avoided.

---

27   (Ecclesiastes 4:9-12)

After a while, Todd began reading the local newspaper. Adopted by a couple as a toddler in China, he was skilled in many languages from traveling extensively with his parents. He became intrigued with an article he was reading, picturing a man in the shadows behind what appeared to be human hearts suspended on a rope. It looked like a wicked ritual of some sort.

Todd attempted to discuss this article with other guests, but they seemed uninterested. The three friends, though, were disconcerted. Francois had an eerie feeling in his gut, but wrote it off to the hype of reporters. He reviewed the events of the day; his adventures with DeShellia, her strange aloofness, the man in the greenhouse, and Todd's stern warning. He also took note that he was rather high, having had more than a few drinks.

Later that evening, there was a dance party next to the high stakes poker club at The Palace. The three friends headed there, attempting to clear their minds while having a little fun. There was not much action on the dance floor, so they went to try their hand at poker, which ended up being a bust. "Guess it's not our night," Francois remarked.

Later in the library over a few drinks, they reconsidered their schedule. Though booked another week at The Palace, they decided to leave early and visit Ireland instead. A unanimous decision and although Francois had high hopes for DeShellia, he knew there were plenty of other beautiful women in the world. A good night's sleep and a pretty face would make him feel brand new.

The next morning, the guys made arrangements at the front desk for transportation back to the city to catch the 5:00 p.m. Coaster ride departing to Ireland. Todd called ahead to secure their lodgings at a hotel he had visited with his family years ago. "There are plenty of fine pubs there along with great music ... and those women," he told his friends.There was more than enough to keep them busy. The opium in China in the region surrounding The Palace slowed life down too much for the young friends, anyhow. One thing they knew, they didn't want to start that stuff. Basketball and college was just a few short weeks ahead. As Tony put it, "Sure, a game is a game, but I'm not about to foul out on the hard stuff."

The other two agreed. Throughout their teens, they had done a lot of things, and too many of their acquaintances had been into a life of goons and drugs. Tony almost went that way himself. If it weren't for his friends; he would be wandering the streets, high, in prison, or dead. The three friends were adventure junkies. "This and that" was OK—but not the hard stuff. Holding each other accountable gave powerful influence to their friendship.

Francois had broken free of many problems because of them. When his buddies saw him ready to blow it, they told him. It was hard to take at first, but repeatedly experiencing the reward of their good advice made it easier to walk away from danger. When Francois stepped back, he could see that those fast girls were fast with others, too. That was fine. He was young, handsome, playful, and they were fun toys. The problem arose when they wanted him to be their toy. His manhood wouldn't stand for that humiliation.

His favorite part was the hunt; the look, being unattainable, pursuing, and of course the best part, catching them. Francois was rarely disappointed. DeShellia had been a fun distraction, but he knew there had to be an Irish beauty waiting for him.

Packed and ready, their driver arrived after lunch to take them to the Coaster. Tossing their bags into the trunk, they hopped into the cab, and were off. Gleeful to escape with just a few losses from the poker table the night before, they set off into their next adventure filled with anticipation. That was the beauty of the game, freedom.

Since their driver spoke no English, they talked about the upcoming school year. Initially it was about basketball, coaches, plays, but over the hours, a shift occurred and they began talking about their goals. Francois wanted to go professional, but the other two wanted to use sports as an opportunity to take them through college. Tony was unclear about his future and figured he'd do the basics the first couple years, and narrow it down later.

Todd, on the other hand, was interested in social issues. His dad was an international politician, and revealed to him issues unknown by many. Todd had a burning desire to make a difference in world politics, wanting to bring hope to those who didn't have any. Because of his dad, Todd as a silent observer sat with many leaders over the years. His dad was a man highly esteemed for his unbiased acceptance and rare ability to keep personal opinions to himself. As a result, Todd received an education of opposing perspectives from the political spectrum.

Todd was idealistic though determined, wanting justice for all, not just a select few. He wanted to model those great human rights activists he had encountered. Though few, men of integrity did exist, for he had met them. He admired their honesty and dedication to equality for all people that went beyond common elitism. Todd fervently hoped that doing this work would help end poverty and oppression. Not a political party man, he saw himself as one in pursuit of justice.

Tony, Todd, and Francois loved to challenge one another's viewpoints, thus necessitating honest self-evaluation. Sure, it was easy to feel a certain way about something, but what about dealing with crisis in the fire of reality? These debates brought the young men great satisfaction while preparing them for the future.

Once they arrived at the Coaster station, they paid their ticket and ascended in a glass elevator to a line awaiting the metal beast. There was a long ramp for the travelers to view the city with its impressive skyline. Vendors asked those waiting in line what they wanted, "Uppers, downers, all arounders." Everyone entered a transported state before the trip. No one would even consider getting on the crazy ride without something to help them along.

Tony, Todd, and Francois realized they were almost totally sober, a first since the beginning of the trip. Tired of the sleepy opium environment they just left, they instead wanted to try something a little perkier, a psychedelic upper that was new on the market. Rush, rush, rush, their brains twirled around in circles. Before long, the Coaster arrived. The door opened and in they went. Once seated, whoosh, they were off-brain rush, body rush, Coaster rush.

When they arrived, they were unable to tell if it took a moment or forever. Time appeared to have no meaning on the Coaster for reality seemed to disappear. Thoughts also faded in and out uncontrollably. Sometimes the question "Why?" arose, but though the reasons were endlessly varied, everything was unimportant. Whenever questions arose, they knew it was time for more sedatives. That was the point—erase the need to question, thus eliminate the pain those questions may cause.

Chapter 26
What Tony Learned in Ireland

Exiting the Coaster, the young men blended with the crowd who just arrived. Immediately they felt the intrigue of Ireland's mysterious, pulsing heartbeat. People often overlooked this aspect of the nation that was forgotten in the Euro struggle. Though the land was fertile, its brown soil ran with eons of spilled blood. Catholic beliefs pulling one arm and Protestant the other created feudal chaos fueled fiery hot over the generations. The result was lost lives of many young men and women, the most valuable of resources, over the ages. The land pulsated so strongly with her history that Francois, Todd and Tony seemed to feel the beat.

Their senses were electric after traveling, heightened by a burning hunger from not eating since noon. There were plenty of cabbies to get them to the next town where their hotel was. When they arrived, their driver waited as they checked in, and then dropped them off at a well-known pub close by.

The next day over brunch they went over the details of the day, thrilled at having included Ireland in their adventure. They would always remember the Coaster as the out-of-body experience that brought them to their senses. While sharing their observations of other passengers, some were dedicated to the rush; to others like themselves, this was a passing experience. All three agreed there would be no more Coaster transports. They would only travel conventional, with no more "little helpers." Those pills were too powerful; they wouldn't allow their life to be overtaken like that.

After finishing the meal, they rented a car, got a map, and set off in search of excitement. Interested in ancient castles, they stopped to visit each one they saw. Reflecting back on Ireland's history, they found it entertaining to share their imaginings regarding what castle life may have been like.

At the end of the day, they decided to try out a local pub for dinner and drinks. Possibly in this quiet town they might stumble on some good local entertainment. If not, they would make their own. Being creative had never been a problem for them. They followed the smell of good food into a small pub filled with locals and laughter. The tables were jammed together with people behaving as if they were at a big celebration. The guys ordered food and beers all around for the patrons. Of course, that made them fast friends with everyone there.

Soon, beer steins were smashing together. With everyone speaking at full volume, Todd, Tony, and Francois were taken into the enchantment of the moment. They asked their new acquaintances questions about Ireland's history, politics, and stories, too. Of course, potatoes and the Loc Ness monster came up, and everyone laughed as the tales kept getting longer.

A story in particular caught the crowd's attention. A hush then came over the room as one of the regulars cleared his throat to share this singsong ditty:

There is a single road all travelers start together, though separate they go.

But soon, O so soon, a fork in the road where a wizened elder set.

His task is to wait and advise, as the denizen travelers come.

For sure enough, all would too early, it seems, stumble upon the free choice they must make.

So on with the tale he was so known to tell.

Of the choice which all men must make?

Left or right, dark or light?

"Which one, O which way," each would cry.

"Well," said the guide, "here's what I've been told, by the few who could return.

The flowery wide path so enchanting it seems would shrink down to brambles and thorns.

But those who chose that way possibly may somehow return from the maze,

O, horrors unknown would exclaim.

The other path, not attractive in the least.

A big tedious hill up; at the top were stones set in a rushing river to pass.

Very few, to none ever returned to tell of what lay ahead—except one chosen by our glorious King

As the next wizened guide to direct.

This narrow, arduous path would lead those courageous ones home to Him instead.

So choose, O dear traveler, choose O so wisely.

For the set of your days are determined with choice.

Don't be deceived by heart-lust, eye or feelings.

Only trust ... what you know to be true.

Come home, come home, come home."

Everyone in the pub sat together in stunned silence. Soon, some of the patrons got up and left with no explanation. As for Todd, Tony, and Francois, they were giddy from all those drinks. Tony suddenly got up, headed to the door and walked out. Todd immediately paid off their tab, and then he and Francois followed Tony out into the clear night.

Meditating on the ditty caused Tony to think about his life and the path he was on. He was standing at a crossroad, and hadn't realized it until then. "I'm the kind of guy who has always done what I wanted," he told himself. "My friends are the best thing in my life; all the times I would have chosen differently but didn't because Todd and Francois wouldn't support those decisions. I need their approval. It wasn't that they always did the right thing, but at least they somehow survived this complex world; in this moment, nothing else matters.

Tony had to settle some things in his heart so instead of heading to the car, he set off toward Brighton Castle where they had stopped earlier that day. It was late, and very still outside; not knowing where they were going or why, Francois and Todd followed Tony. The three young men journeyed up and down hills and valleys as a dense mist rolled in.

As they approached Brighton Castle, there was a flash of light that caused Tony to fall face first to the ground. Todd and Francois stumbled and fell, too.

"Where am I?" Tony asked. Neither of his friends answered. Though hardly aware of them earlier while climbing up and down the hills, Tony looked around, but they seemed to have completely vanished. Suddenly it was daytime, and he was walking with his Father in a small Irish town.

Instead of cars, horse-drawn carts bounced over cobblestone roads as they walked together. They talked about a variety of topics, periodically stopping so his Father could point something out as they went. There were many people out enjoying the sunny afternoon, wherever they were.

Tony was especially interested in the beautiful girls surrounding him laughing and talking with eyes flashing as they spoke. Each passing girl was lovelier than the last. His Father became quiet so Tony could focus all his attention on the parade of lovelies passing by. One girl was very alluring; curly long red locks tumbled down her shoulders and past her waist. She wore a soft green cotton dress that showed off her perfect figure. She wore black button-up boots of an era long past. So inviting were her looks and smile, but just as he was about to speak to her, another girl even more lovely began vying for his attention. One by one they walked by, each more beautiful than the last, seemingly for his exclusive enjoyment. In all his days, he had never seen so many beautiful girls in one place.

For some reason Tony couldn't talk to them, so they got bored and walked away. His attention shifted as loud voices came from a pub a few doors down. Two massive men hauled out a drunk fellow, throwing him down on the sidewalk right in front of him. The man's shirt was stained from hard drinking and his pants were soiled. Right before the man lost consciousness, the two of them exchanged looks. Panic shot through Tony, for *this man looked just like him.* Immediately everything faded and Tony returned to the present with the memory of that drunken man's eyes haunting him.

Tony got up and continued walking toward Brighton Castle, a magnificent building surrounded by a rock wall. In the distance, flocks of sheep dotting the hills around the castle were being guided by a Shepherd. The Shepherd was singing softly to the sheep contentedly munching on the lush green grass. Above the entrance to the castle were carved these words:

"The kingdom of the world has
become the kingdom of our
LORD and of his Christ,
and he will reign for ever and ever."[28]

Tony and his Father— at least the person with him who acted as if he were Tony's Father—walked up a cobblestone path to a massive front door and were greeted by a stately butler who opened the door before they could knock. He led them to a garden room set and ready with tea and cakes for the two of them as a cozy fire burned in the fireplace driving out the chill.

What is happening? Tony asked himself. This is not my childhood home. As for the man who is my Father, he is very different than the dad I know.

The butler waited for the two men to sit down to pour the tea, then left the room. Tony waited silently for his Father to speak as they sipped the tea. Finally, his Father said,

"Remember those beautiful girls and how they all wanted you? Each more attractive than the last; exciting, alluring, making you desire them more and more although you couldn't speak to them. Though wanting to touch them, you could only look. What was going through your mind?"

What is happening? Tony could not get his mind around the questions his Father asked. His Father had never spoken to him this way before, but had always been the kind of guy who remained distant. The only conversations they ever had were how Tony was a good-for-nothing and wouldn't do anything with his life. Even excelling in school and sports, his dad wouldn't acknowledge those successes.

---

28   In the book of Revelation 11:15.

All he saw was every flaw and failing Tony had magnified a hundred times over.

Tony had quit listening to his dad years ago; it was just safer that way. Once in middle school he brought home a girl—not for an honorable introduction. He actually thought his parents were out, since the car wasn't parked in the drive. It wasn't until later did he learn the car was in the shop being repaired. Anyway, he and this girl had just finished a snack in the kitchen and were heading upstairs to his bedroom when his dad came out of the den, surprising them all.

Angry words ensued. His dad made degrading comments toward the girl, and then started slapping Tony. Instinctively, Tony balled up his fists and the two men, father and son, entered a full-scale brawl. Somehow it ended. Tony's nose was not broken, but blood had splattered all over the two of them. His dad's eye immediately turned black and swelled up, while the girl screamed hysterically the whole time. Pointing to the front door his dad yelled, "Get out and don't come back!"

So he did. With no intention of returning, he went to stay with Francois. Tony's mom showed up after school the next day crying and begging him to come home, which he did reluctantly for her sake. He and his dad didn't look at each other for months. They finally grunted at one another, but the girl and the fight weren't ever talked about again.

That was the way things were at his place. After that, Tony found other ways to connect with girls that didn't involve his dad. Tony eventually developed such an impenetrable wall, his dad could yell in his face and he wouldn't even hear him. It was almost like having on his headphones. These well-learned survival skills with the "dad detach" button was always set to "on"—nothing could come in.

"What is happening?" This time Tony asked aloud.

His Father replied, "Son, I want to heal you. That is why I have shown you these things so we can talk about them. I understand you are in shock. I know your experience with your earthly dad has been difficult. That is why I brought you here. Are you willing to open your wounded heart and be honest with Me and yourself?"

Tony took some time to decide if he was willing to answer the questions, let alone feel.

His Father said, "This is going to be painful, so take your time and count the cost. Just know you can trust Me, for I have your very best in mind."

Tony figured, what can I lose? Unsure if this was reality or fantasy, he chose to answer the questions thoroughly. His Father seemed to be familiar with what was inside Tony's heart as He repeated the first question.

"Remember those beautiful girls, what were you thinking? Why did you want them?"

Tony responded, "I knew they would make me feel good, maybe even happy." After a moment he added, "They made me feel wanted as a virile man. Powerful, and I like the way that feels."

Then his Father asked, "How did you feel when they disappeared?"

At that Tony said, "Shocked and sad. I asked myself, 'Why does this keep happening to me? Whenever a great opportunity comes along, why does it seem to always slip away?' Just like those women, they were a great opportunity."

Once the thought was completed in his mind, Tony started to get angry. He wondered would he ever know the love of a good woman, or just the touch of many. Then he remembered the drunken man that had been thrown out of the tavern. That bothered him because Tony didn't have any brothers, yet that man looked just like him. Terrified, he remembered his own body was saturated with drugs and alcohol.

It was all so painful he started to weep. He felt his past colliding into the present, causing an emotional explosion inside of him prompted by both the visions and piercing questions. The tears soon turned into screams, then heaving sobs as emotion flooded over him; fear, panic, sorrow, shame, grief.

Before he knew what happened, his Father picked him up and held him as though Tony were a little baby. Now Tony was crying uncontrollably as the dam of emotions broke and poured out; a lifetime of pain and loss.

As Tony began to calm down, he could faintly hear this song:

"Do not be afraid, little flock, for your Father has been pleased to give you the kingdom."[29]

Tony looked up to see the Shepherd who had been outside, standing before him. He was the one who was singing. The Father instructed Tony, "Follow the Shepherd down the way a bit until you hear laughter and conversation. Knock on the door of that house and go in. There is a man there whose name is Morgan, and he will explain these things to you. Tell him your Father sent you to meet the King."

Tony left the castle speechless, following the Shepherd. Brought to the point of mental, emotional, and physical crisis with thoughts swirling around at such an intense pace he didn't know where to start. Then, in the blink of an eye, he was back out on the moors, lying face down again on the cold wet grass next to Todd and Francois, sobbing. This song floated in the air.

O holy Shepherd of the sheep
Who run away, astray, wholeheartedly from You.
What sorrow, loss and long-suffering you endure
Waiting, ever waiting for us.
All lambs and sheep alike.
No respecter of "sheeps," persons
Such love, ah, such love
Incomprehensible
Lavished and overflowing as volumes of the ocean deep
To fill a tiny thimble—us.
Your ability, our capacity.
How do you do it?
It rips us apart.
We get a glimpse.
Still, we run away and hide.
But one day—how?
I don't know how.

29   Luke 12:32.

You penetrate our thick wall of defense.
Down to the real—the raw You go.
Addressing free will
You woo and romance.
"Come back, little sheep,
Is it yet enough the price you pay for your ways?
I am calling, little sheep.
Listen."
"He who has an ear, let him hear what the Spirit says to the churches."[30]

Filled with sorrow, Tony was sobbing with emotion. His friends looked at him, shocked. Though knowing him many years, they'd never experienced anything like this with him, or with anyone else for that matter.

"Maybe you never really know a man," Todd mumbled. "Complicated, this sin-sick world we live in. There are always predators. The way of creation, one eating another, not always physically, so is the pecking order of life. But people everywhere are hurting. Such sin-sickness among the masses, with multitudes plagued by emptiness."[31]

As Tony lay on the damp ground, thoughts of that extraordinary journey ran through his head. The "stuff" is the easy way out of pain, but where is the Game Master now? He offers only distractions for solutions, sedatives that keep us from having to feel. *Now that I am stripped raw inside, these games seem so trite and shallow. Who can handle all these challenges? We must have a Warrior—a mighty valiant leader to guide and lead us through the war zone of life.*

Tony arose from the moors no longer broken. Instead, his eyes burned with a fierce determination to follow his Father's instruction. He must follow, for his very life depended upon doing so.

His brain was now clear, not foggy as when they left the pub. The full moon was glowing in the night sky directly overhead. Todd and Francois attempted to guide Tony back to the car but soon

30 Revelation 2:7.
31 Todd is quoting Pastor David Wilkerson of Times Square Church in New York.

realized that wasn't going to work. Tony continued to press on into the unknown as he mumbled something incoherent. Todd started to feel uncomfortable as he remembered the alarming newspaper article he read in China. They sure didn't want to meet up with the likes of anything like that! Was it possible the same evil resided in this country, too?

Trailing behind Tony, they heard in the distance sounds of people gathered together in laughter and animated conversation. Though faint at first, the noise became louder with each step as they continued stumbling in that direction.

Chapter 27
Morgan and Ariel Welcome the Travelers

Morgan and Ariel were having a housewarming party in their new home that was situated with a view of the water. Wisdom and the King were there, comfortably enjoying their friends. It was an exciting celebration; everyone was having a wonderful time.

Morgan and Ariel left their guests and went into their bedroom, a grand room with picture windows overlooking the water. They sat down, blissfully talking, as only twenty-one years of marriage allows, and then Morgan began kissing Ariel.

They were interrupted when someone opened the glass door in the other room, accompanied by crashing noises. Morgan and Ariel got up to see what was going on. There, in the midst of their celebration stood three young strangers who were noticeably drunk. The sober guests were stunned, silently looking at each other and the young men.

Morgan assessed the situation, consulting briefly with the King, and then took decisive action. "What are your names?" he inquired.

After brief introductions, Tony spoke about his recent experience with the Father. Morgan and Ariel led the unexpected visitors to a sitting room to speak more comfortably as they continued to sober up.

When Tony began speaking about his meeting with the Shepherd, everyone paid attention. He told this fascinating tale: After they left the pub, the era changed to sometime in the late 1600s. He and his Father were walking through the moors among royal castles. At a certain point they stopped and his Father became serious. He requested before Tony got married that he introduce his yet unknown fiancé to the family. He also stressed the importance of remaining sexually pure until marriage.

The conversation had been very deep and meaningful, but was certainly not one that ever occurred with his real dad.

This only made the earlier experience more puzzling. Who was that Father out there in the moors? He sure wasn't the man he had known all his life. And to cry like that, Tony couldn't remember doing so since childhood when his dad told him to stop because "big boys don't cry."

"I've always been strong, silent, tough, not emotional. I've been taught since a young age to restrain my feelings, or dad would give me a reason to cry. But out in the haze, everything became clear. I know I experienced a Power much greater than I've ever known. Certainly a Power greater than me, caused me to fall face-down like a dead man," Tony stated. He continued, saying that the Father clearly told him to come and speak with Morgan.

Todd and Francois listened closely as the story of the recent happenings unfolded. Though seemingly obscure events, it seemed they were orchestrated by some hidden Power. That is why they were here, because this Unknown Force told Tony the King wanted to meet him.

The King then approached Tony, looked him in the eye, and asked, "Are you ready to lay down your life, take up My cross and follow Me?"

Without hesitation, Tony responded, "Yes."

Tony spoke of his past that had been filled with lies and deceit, producing hurts, habits, and hang-ups. By now it was very late and most of the guests had left, but not Tony and Morgan. They remained with the King in intimate conversation, experiencing His abundant healing.

At one point in their conversation, the King presented Tony with a very powerful sword like the one David took from Goliath before cutting off his head. "For the word of God is living and active. Sharper than any double-edged sword, it penetrates even to dividing soul and spirit, joints and marrow; it judges the thoughts and attitudes of the heart,"[32] the King promised.

---

32   (Hebrews 4:12).

Though he tried, Tony could hardly lift the sword off the ground because it was so heavy and he was unskilled. Morgan told Tony as he read from the Holy Word, his ability to use the sword would improve. "The King certainly has a powerful word to release through you, but you must prepare for it," Morgan said. As the darkness of the night gave way to the dawn, the King asked Tony to wait on Him, learn his ways, and be transformed into His mighty warrior. Tony readily agreed.

When Tony arrived at the hotel the next day, he shared what had happened with his two friends, who had left Morgan's house earlier that morning. They were intrigued, but unsure what to do with the information. Since planning to stay at the hotel for a while, Tony took the opportunity to learn how to use the sword he had received. He got battered and scarred in the process, but soon became agile with the powerful weapon. Not sure how to use it yet, he chose to trust the King with what lay ahead.

Later that week, the three friends invited Morgan to join them for the day. As they walked through a wooded area, Tony saw a red serpent with piercing eyes looking straight at him about a hundred yards away. The serpent unexpectedly lunged, bit him, and then returned to his hiding place. Although dazed, Tony realized how the serpent's subtlety and speed overcame him. A few moments later, the serpent peered from its hiding place, attempting to strike again. Tony was ready this time. Drawing his sharp sword he ran full speed toward the vicious creature, and cut off its head, then stomped out the remaining life left in its gruesome body in order to protect the others from harm. "The Word of God is the Sword of the Spirit," Tony said with growing confidence.

Chapter 28
Time to Travel Onward

The time had come for the three adventurers to say goodbye to Morgan and Ariel. Though a strong bond of friendship had grown between them and the King, their travels with the Game Master were not finished. Tony set his heart to follow Wisdom through the remainder of the game, continuing for the sake of his friends, only now he followed a different voice.

Hither and yon they went to many exciting places, as the Master's brushstrokes to His living masterpiece drew them into unimaginable delights. He revealed what a privilege life was with all its beauty wherever they went. From South America's lush jungles, to historic Europe, the diversity of Asia, into the mysterious Middle East ... yet one experience was most memorable. This is what happened:

The three young men arrived at a marshy flatland in the countryside. Nearby was a rock quarry that had been cut out by machinery years ago, but had become overgrown with brambles and wild things. Other people were visiting there, too, but weren't close enough to chat with. The guys hiked a trail to an upper plateau, which opened into a remote field with an absolutely breathtaking view!

As they continued, the land began cracking at the edges as though it were a thin sheet of ice on a frozen lake. They noticed the land was changing into crystal clear water filled with beautiful fish. They heard someone say, "Watch for the goldfish." As they looked, the land began to turn into water, and strangely the three travelers were swimming with the fish.

A little girl goldfish swam up to them and started chattering, carrying a little flag device with interchangeable signs under one of her fins. When the three friends asked what it was for, she became nervous. They continued to press the issue, so she told them about a mean man who had her heart suspended on a rope along with a bunch of other hearts. If she didn't find souls for him, he would play a deadly game of shoot the goldfish with her. Unless there was someone to gather the tortured creatures up and gently put them into the King's healing pool, they would die a slow and painful death. The mean man tortured his hostages if they didn't play by his rules, or when he tired of them, whichever came first.

The girl goldfish was terrified she had revealed the situation to them. "I don't want to be like this anymore," she confessed. "I ask your forgiveness as well as forgiveness from all the souls I helped capture for the man, and repent for harming so many unsuspecting victims."

Just then, a vicious-looking metal fish composed of wire mesh swam toward them with great speed. It had neither skin nor organs, only wire mesh with water flowing through its blowfish shaped body. Its mouth was metal with vicious looking teeth that were used to cut open the skulls of its victims, extracting the brain from behind, and taking it to the Game Master. The little goldfish's job was to identify the victims by category with a little flag so the collection process went smoothly. The captured brain was then fully owned by the Game Master, and the creature's body had to obey him.

As she told her story, the metal fish came within inches from Todd's brain. Suddenly some holy beings gathered around him with a trap fitted perfectly to lock the fish's mouth. They successfully captured the metal fish and disarmed it. Tony, Todd and Francoise realized these warriors who had rescued them were two women of great spiritual stature. They were amazed how Todd had been rescued from that terrible fate. Immediately Todd, Francoise, and the girl goldfish cried out to the King and repented fully of their selfish ways.

The women warriors told them about a place called Greenwater, where the life-giving water brought tremendous healing. Tony had heard about this place, and was grateful his friends wanted to go there. It was hidden away and if Wisdom hadn't led them, they never would have found it.

On they traveled into new territory, almost faltering at the mud flats if Wisdom had not intervened. Arriving at the Living Water, they jumped into the effervescent pool so pure it was actually *alive*!

There they met up with Morgan and Ariel, who encouraged them to plunge in and drink.

Todd had been quiet about the King up until then from a heavy burden that he had carried his whole life. This private pain caused him to make many wrong choices in the past, but when he jumped in the pool, something miraculous occurred. Tearfully he related the experience:

"I saw the King, bare-chested," Todd said. "With my fists balled up, and completely enraged, I repeatedly beat His chest screaming, 'I hate you, I hate you, I hate you!' The King quietly stood while I spat accusations at Him such as, 'how could you do this to me, how could you allow this happen?' When my anger was spent, I slumped over in exhaustion.

"The King lifted my face to His, looked directly into my eyes, and said, 'I am not your enemy. Whatever you went through, I went through also. I will never leave nor forsake you. I was there all the time, and always will be; as I am even now.'"

Todd told them his life with all its pain and torment was set straight in an instant. He was no longer bitter or resentful. As for the addictions and sin, everything was washed away. The King had healed his soul.

Chapter 29
Bridge Heaven

"Believing in fairies won't keep Tinker Bell alive."

After resting awhile at Greenwater, Morgan and Ariel ventured deeper into the wilderness, trusting Wisdom to build greater maturity in them through the process. They began those first few steps away from the Game Master initially focusing upon imps, trolls, and gremlins. They imagined the entry over Greenwater into Bridge Heaven housed trolls, but later realized they were only boisterous young travelers. Greeted by a young family at the entrance, Morgan and Ariel inquired about the path before them. The young wife, filled with joy at her family's experience on the path, urged them on while sharing points of interest.

From her encouragement, Morgan and Ariel decided to pay no attention to the tricks of the Game Master but trust Wisdom instead. Wisdom said, "Keep your mind focused on Me." Each step their confidence grew as they communed with Wisdom and one another. Within a short time, it seemed everything had changed from darkness into light. Though Morgan and Ariel had chosen Wisdom years earlier and diligently served Him, this new journey would help to seal their commitment to seek the King for who He is, not what they could get from Him.

They were led to this remote place, a passageway many travelers used about a century ago, by Wisdom. Over the years settlers built huge cities along the route that caused the land to prosper agriculturally. Soon the nation moved past the gold rush, then the Industrial Age, into the present era of technology.

Those travelers were as diverse in their motivations then as now. Some lusted after plunder gained by heeding the voice of the Game

Master. Others communed with Wisdom, experiencing unconditional love from the King, which they passed on to others in that generation.

After considering these matters, Morgan and Ariel took their first step into the rugged wilderness. What a change—the ground seemed to invite them in, while the air was filled with the sweet fragrance of cedar and pine. A rushing river flowed by as they hiked up the mountain. It was one of those perfect sunny days that seemed like all creation had invited them to celebrate the Creator together.

They could have ventured on further. Instead, they walked slowly, stopping often to absorb the magnificence of this place where it seemed all the creatures were in perfect harmony.

Coming to the first manmade bridge, they stopped halfway across to survey the surroundings. The water rushed beneath, swirling in an enchanting blue-green lagoon that exited into a waterfall. "That little lagoon is the kind of place you imagine mermaids dwell," Ariel marveled.

Morgan and Ariel waited, hoping to spot one. Other travelers had spoken of knowing a friend of a friend that had seen a mermaid before, though neither Morgan nor Ariel had. After waiting with no success, land lovers as they were, they remarked to each other that they really didn't want to meet a mermaid. Mermaids enjoyed the water and probably wouldn't want to be tempted to cross into Morgan's and Ariel's world, where they did not belong.

This is not much different than our own friendships and the powerful influence they have upon us, Morgan reflected. He thought about how his associations had either brought him closer to Wisdom and the King, where he belonged, or they led him away to the Game Master.

Ariel said softly, "I'm thinking how, like the mermaids, we have our own world with its many freedoms. They must dwell in water to survive, but aren't limited like that, instead getting to choose our own way."

Morgan turned to Ariel and hugged her before crossing the bridge. Suddenly something captured his attention. On the river's bank below were some animal prints he could not identify. Though the place was called "Horse Ford," this crossing had obviously been passed by more than just horses. There was evidence the mysterious creatures ran in herds along with elephants, lions, bears, leopards, and other wild creatures.

They crossed the bridge as clusters of fairies, butterflies, and birds of various colors followed. In the water were shy turtles along with attractive fish. The whole area was teeming with health at this fresh source of living water. Whoever chose to drink of this water, Wisdom bestowed great strength on them.

Desiring travelers to partake, Wisdom invited all to "come and drink deeply." Morgan and Ariel gladly accepted the invitation. Immediately He opened the door to reveal truth about His Word that was formerly hidden to them both individually and as lifelong travelers. He encouraged them to cast off burdens, habits, and deceptions they had picked up, and instead equip for the battles which lay just ahead.

Wisdom revealed how chosen paths along with various methods of travel gave their own unique rewards. Though there were many travel options, the King chose the one best suited for each situation; whether elephants, horses, leopards, fairies or even mermaids. Included were flying contraptions, and water vessels of all sorts, along with other land, air, or sea vehicles.

At this crossroad, Wisdom asked them to commit to His ways, denying anything that may draw them away. He instructed them to search their hearts and count the cost, since Kingdom issues require following the King daily. He said, "The cross is the only building material you will ever need. That is the major difference between Me and the Game Master. Travel light. People need trust and faith while heeding Me, whereas the Game Master heaps issues to habit upon stuff to habit upon lust, indefinitely."

Wisdom went on to explain that was why the Game Master's followers need vast storage space, to protect the attainment of their plunder. The rich have their own great dwelling places, fancy toys, and sophisticated travel devices, storing everything in many layers. Once having attained their potential, they often squander it on selfish pleasure. Even the destitute have carts loaded to the top as they attempt to satisfy unquenchable cravings.

"The lust for more steadily intensifies according to whatever 'more' is to an individual. Attempting to turn from the allurement of the Game Master, many can't, for he drives them mercilessly. On the other hand, the King has many gifts for us—far beyond our comprehension to choose from—some visible, some invisible from another realm."

Morgan and Ariel noticed on either side of the wilderness bridge were many fallen travelers. How they had become paralyzed was a grievous matter, and it was especially difficult to behold them in such torment. These were victims of their own self-seeking satisfaction. The Game Master enticed them and they had become hollow shells; last gaspers destined for "those" institutions, if not already there—"You know, the sanitariums, hospitals and prisons," Wisdom said. Death was inevitable, produced by a life poorly spent.

The common terms describing the devastation were familiar: *addiction* and *co-dependency*. Unfortunately, people become obsolete, not for lack of ability, rather, from heeding the wrong voice. Wisdom told Morgan and Ariel to be alert, showing them how to intervene with love and speak life instead.

"You know," continued Wisdom, "Hearing Me, or shall I say learning to hear Me, requires patience mixed with honesty, open-mindedness, and willingness. These attributes, if not acquired at a young age, are learned through the school of hard knocks. The number of souls who refuse to surrender to sound wisdom is incomprehensible. The result is devastating. Unfortunately, depending on how the Game Master has colored it, most travelers end up blaming the King for the disaster.

"'How could He allow these things to happen,' some say and, "If He was so great, He would rescue us." Others said, "What about the innocent victims, young children and even babies? It is painful to see how small choices cause such huge consequences," Wisdom concluded.

Morgan and Ariel had come close to disaster on many occasions. They washed their overworked hearts in the Living Water. Wisdom graciously opened their ears, removed the scales from their eyes, rescued them from complacency and gave them new hearts of flesh. It was amazing that serving the King over the years, though satisfying in many ways, still brought painful experiences. Though walking with Him, they sorely needed refreshment.

In the midst of the healing, with lifted hands they gave a shout of gratitude to *all* Wisdom had accomplished. Morgan and Ariel soaked in this training that drew them to walk more intimately with the King and rescue the perishing. Numerous faces flashed by as they became equipped for the future. They more clearly understood why some people receive Wisdom's instruction yet refuse to be rescued. Choosing Wisdom was not the result of either goodness or intelligence, but rather a soul's dependence on the King. This comforting realization drew them to Wisdom's guidance on behalf of Todd, Tony, and Francois. Morgan revealed the story of Todd to Ariel—how long ago in Asia, Morgan and some other followers of the King had rescued Todd and located adoptive parents for him when he was still a child.

After hiking a while, Morgan and Ariel stopped to rest. Watching from a rock overhang, they observed the three young men in the valley below washing the filth from the world in the Living Waters just as they had recently done. Morgan and Ariel walked toward them, asking what Wisdom would have them say about the Kingdom of Light. After encouraging Todd, Tony and Francois, Morgan and Ariel resumed their journey.

Wisdom led them deeper into this uncharted place, revealing important lessons on how to reach hurting people. He told about His love for all travelers, especially the young, for that is the best time to choose Him; time and opportunity is on their side. Once doing so, they may become who they were meant to be. "Even a tiny connection with Me is enough of an intervention to protect them from great destruction," said Wisdom.

As Morgan and Ariel continued walking, they arrived at the Forest of the Young Ones. There they observed how elders were involved in teaching the young about the King. Wisdom revealed how, unfortunately, the needs of the young increase while the demands of our society causes people to focus more on themselves. Often the young are forgotten. The number of the abused, neglected, and abandoned continue growing at alarming rates, while those responding to the needs become less and less. "The work is very demanding with long hours and uncertain future which appears to have little reward (at least in this realm) to this 'me-more' generation," Wisdom said with great sorrow. "But the King wants to reveal that He is the Advocate."

Morgan understood, for he had grown up as practically an orphan himself. Over the years he was determined to be involved directly with the young to see they were cared for properly.

"My desire is that Elders are involved with youth in creative ways in response to Me," advised Wisdom. "Tell them to open their ears, hearts, minds, pocketbooks, and time-clocks. Our young ones need the elderly to spend time loving and caring for them. The lessons learned from the Elders of the Forest of the Young will bring untold satisfaction in living with full reliance on Me," encouraged Wisdom.

Morgan and Ariel continued through the wilderness as Wisdom taught and filled them with joy. Early on they were mostly alone, but as the day progressed they met other travelers. Though the path was becoming narrow and difficult to find, they had confidence once established firmly in Wisdom, the tedious way becomes the best route to travel into the King's territory.

They carried this promise with them: "Continue in the daily challenge to trust and follow the King that when the chosen day arrives, they would cross the final bridge victoriously to enter the very gates of Heaven."

A Note from the Author

Dear Reader,

I hope you have enjoyed the story of Morgan and Ariel's life entwined with the King.

If you have any comments, or are interested in other books I have written, check out my web-site at:

www.NormaLuciano.com

Though pilgrims and strangers here, may we encourage one another along the path to our eternal home.

Blessings,
Norma